MRS CRAGGS

Mrs Craggs

Crimes Cleaned Up

H.R.F. Keating

BUCHAN & ENRIGHT, PUBLISHERS
LONDON

First published in 1985 by
Buchan & Enright, Publishers, Limited
53 Fleet Street, London EC4Y 1BE

British Library Cataloguing in Publication Data

Keating, H.R.F.
  Mrs. Craggs: crimes cleaned up.
  I. Title
  823'.914[F]   PR6061.E26

ISBN 0 907675 48 4

Photoset in North Wales by
Derek Doyle & Associates, Mold, Clwyd
Printed and bound in Great Britain by
Redwood Burn Ltd., Trowbridge, Wiltshire.

The story 'Mrs Craggs Sings a Different Tune' is an adapted extract from the author's
novel *Death of a Fat God*, first published by Collins in 1963.

CONTENTS

Contents

AUTHOR'S NOTE

Reading over the stories I have gathered together (and rearranged a bit) for this volume, I was struck by the fearful liberties I took, when I first wrote them, with various august institutions in which many of them were set. Not only did I, twice at least, alter the very order of Nature, once even in that holy of holies the Chelsea Physic Garden, but I also wantonly traduced the holders of the most important offices in the land. So let me say now that the Person who figures in a Garden Party at somewhere not unlike Buckingham Palace is not, of course, any living monarch or any previous one. Nor is the man shown as being editor of the greatest newspaper in the world in any way any of the distinguished journalists who have edited, with various ups and downs, *The Times*.

In fact, none of the characters appearing in these pages is intended to represent any person living or dead.

I

MRS CRAGGS AND THE LORDS SPIRITUAL AND TEMPORAL

IT WAS A FUNNY THING, Mrs Craggs used to say about the cleaning job she once had at the House of Lords, but, in spite of it all being so hoity-toity, there was always a lot of what you might call capers. Nothing nasty, mind. Well, not until That Day. But definitely capers.

Things like the great writing-paper row. Between the Bishop of Porchester, that was, and Tryulph, fourteenth Earl Balerno and Gosforth. Well, that was the name that Mr Holofernes, the Attendant whose domain coincided with Mrs Craggs's, always used for him. Every time. The whole lot.

Mrs Craggs called him Lord Bally Earn Oh. And sometimes to his face. Because he was one of the few peers she ever had dealings with, seeing that her work in the place – carpets hoovered and surrounds polished, general tidying and everything else dusted and rubbed till it shone – was done in the mornings while their noble lordships did their work – revising Bills sent from the House of Commons, starting up a few quiet Bills of their own and general debating at a high moral level – in the afternoons of Tuesdays, Wednesdays and Thursdays. But Lord Balerno and Gosforth was a particularly sleepy little peer curling up like a rabbit on the red leather benches of the chamber during debates and quite often tucking himself away in a corner and being found only next morning by Mrs Craggs as she went about her work. That was the way she had got to know him.

And an old fuss-pot he was, she used to tell her friend Mrs Milhorne who had charge of the next set of committee rooms at that time – and her polish not a patch on mine, Mrs Craggs used to think, but not say – always on about waste and things not being in their place and people 'misusing' this and that. 'Misusing' was a favourite word of Lord Balerno's. And 'misusing' was what he had accused the Bishop of Porchester of in the great writing-paper row.

Well, of course, Mrs Craggs said to Mrs Milhorne, that old Lord Spiritual had asked for it. The way he went on.

Yes, Mrs Milhorne agreed rather doubtfully, 'it don't seem right to be so sort of desperate. Well, not for a Bishop.'

'Desperate,' Mrs Craggs replied with a sniff. 'Pig-headed's what I call it. Downright pig-headed, he is, that old Bish. Why, he'd call black white if he thought it was red, and well you know it.'

The Bishop of Porchester, indeed, had been nominated to his see many years before during the full flow of a Labour Government, and with the passing of time his opinions had, if anything, become more Left-wing than ever. And it had been a very Left-wing letter to a newspaper written on House of Lords writing-paper which had been the cause of the trouble between himself and the fourteenth Earl Balerno and Gosforth, otherwise Old Bally Earn Oh.

Often, as Mrs Craggs, her day's work done, made her way out through the lofty spaces of St Stephen's Hall – Mr Holofernes, who seldom missed a chance of imparting information of an edifying character, could never refer to the hall without pointing out that it had been behind the statue there of the great Edmund Burke, 'that hincomparable horator', that the maniac Bellingham had lurked in the year 1812 before striking down Spencer Perceval, 'twenty-first Prime Minister' – she used to say to herself that the old House of Lords was at least always good for a bit a laugh. It was as

10

nice a job that way as she'd ever had, except for the too often looming presence of Mr Holofernes in his statutory black tail-suit with that big gold medallion dangling under his long solemn face and his way of looking down his nose and loosing off 'a whole lot of stuff as you'd rather not be put to the trouble o' remembering'.

All the same, Mrs Milhorne would say when Mrs Craggs stated her opinion of Mr Holofernes, 'all the same he has give his life to the House. You can't deny that.' She would sigh then. A great gusty sigh, from right down in the depths of her soul. 'I think I may give my life to something,' she would add. 'Only, o' course, there's me health.'

'Well, this ain't getting no dusting done,' Mrs Craggs would quickly bang in then. She had heard a great deal in her time about Mrs Milhorne's health.

Yes, she thought as she set to work putting a bit of good old elbow-grease on to the tops of the low cupboards that ran along one wall of Committee Room F, it's all very well giving your life to a place, but that don't entitle you to tell everyone time and again that the Lord Chancellor sits on the Woolsack when presiding over the House, 'but does not hact in the capacity of Chairman, the House conducting its business without a Chair.' All standing up, I suppose, Mrs Craggs liked to mutter then. And as for that big red leather pouffe, as she called the Woolsack after she had been taken from her regular duties once to work in the Chamber itself, well, what if it was 'filled with samples of wool from all parts of the hempire'? There hadn't been an empire, not what you could call an empire, for years. And a good job too. High and mightying it over all those poor natives.

Nor did 'giving your life' to a place entitle you every time Lord Pinnington, who was a regular old barrel of lard, came waddling and wheezing by to recall at length that once when Lord Norris and Lord Grey were tellers and Lord Norris, 'being subject to vapours', was not paying attention, Lord Grey had counted a particularly corpulent peer as ten lords and so a Bill had been passed that never should have been. Or, every time the Marquess of Middlehampton came to the House (which was very often) to go on about how that peer – mad as a hatter, he was, Mrs Craggs knew well – had had the distinction of having another peer 'move that the clerk at the Table do read the horder of the House relating to asperity of speech against him, an event that hoccurs hardly once in your average lifetime.'

Mrs Craggs never let all that stop her getting on with her work, even though Mr Holofernes seemed to find plenty of time to stand about loosing off. But then he had a way with the House that was all his own – perhaps because of the life he had given to it – extending right down to what was served in the Lords Refreshment Rooms. 'We have a particular fine Madeira wine, Mrs C, the like of which, as I can vouch for, you will not find helsewhere.'

Yes, there were some capers that went on. And when it came to tidying up of a morning, there were some funny things she had found lying about too. Once a live hen, 'sitting there quiet as you please, clucking away like she owned the place'. That had proved to be a notion of waddling old Lord Pinnington's who had wanted to make a point when someone had 'moved for papers on the agricultural question', only fellow peers had luckily dissuaded him from actually taking the fowl into the Chamber. And often enough there were small paper bags of Nuttall's Mintoes. Those always had to be returned to Lord Middlehampton as quickly as possible before he exploded into one of his rages again. And another time there had been a Kalashnikov machine rifle, courtesy of the Bishop of Porchester. And not once but twice there had been little wash-leather bags containing a number of gold sovereigns. And no one had ever claimed either of those. But the most surprising thing of all Mrs Craggs ever found was on one Wednesday morning. The Wednesday she ever afterwards thought of as That Day.

She had been delayed by a series of small mishaps and had not managed to get into Committee Room F until about eleven o'clock, when she really should have been already on her way home. So she had scurried round with her preliminary tidying-up, but when she had got to the row of low cupboards running all along one wall under a big gloomy picture of one of the Lords Chancellor in voluminous robes and dusty-looking full-bottomed grey wig she had caught a strong whiff of peppermint. Another of his little old bags, she had thought, and had whipped open the sliding door of the cupboard. Only to find Tryulph, fourteenth Earl Balerno and Gosforth. And this time he was not sleeping but very plainly murdered.

What a kerfuffle there had been. Mrs Craggs had, quick as you like, slammed the cupboard door across again and had gone to look for somebody to break the news to. Unfortunately who should be almost immediately outside the door of Committee Room F but Mr Holofernes, black tail-suit, dangling gold medallion, long solemn face and all. So Mrs Craggs had told him. Which turned out to be a fair mistake. Because Mr Holofernes, having first alluded briefly to the assassination of Spencer Perceval, 'twenty-first Prime Minister', took it into his head that the matter would have to be dealt with by the Serjeant-at-Arms and by no one else.

'Get the police,' Mrs Craggs said. 'Phone the Yard and quick about it. This is murder. Someone's been killed.'

'A peer of the realm has been done to —' Mr Holofernes began to correct her argumentatively.

'Get the police,' said Mrs Craggs.

And Mr Holofernes went then, suddenly meek as a lamb, to the nearest telephone and dialled 230 1212. And he passed on the message to such effect, too, that in less than a quarter of an hour two gentlemen from Scotland Yard were entering Committee Room F.

By that time, too, of course, various other people had arrived, summoned chiefly by Mr Holofernes, restored again to his customary state of dignity. There was the Serjeant-at-Arms, who was a retired Air Vice-Marshal. There was the Staff Superintendent, who was a retired Lieutenant-Commander. There was the Yeoman Usher of the Black Rod, who was a retired Naval Captain. There was the Gentleman-Usher of the Black Rod, who was a retired Lieutenant-General. And there was – nobody quite knew why – the Examiner of Private Acts, who was a lady barrister of formidable intelligence given to

13

wearing little green hats. And half a dozen other people of much less consequence, including Mrs Craggs and her friend Mrs Milhorne.

'Now then,' said the first of the Scotland Yard gentlemen, a tall man with a face almost as lugubrious as that of Mr Holofernes, dressed in a dark blue suit of ferocious respectability. 'Now then, where might I find this alleged body? And who might be the person who made the initial discovery?'

And that brought Mrs Craggs, who had been standing near the door wondering whether she ought to slip quietly out and wait somewhere else, to the fore once again. She made her way over to the fatal cupboard.

'It's here, Superintendent,' she said, deciding that that exalted rank, read about often enough in her study of juicy murders in the papers, must be about right. 'Here, in this old cupboard, Superintendent.'

'Sergeant, if you please,' said the man with the dark blue suit. 'Detective-Sergeant Browne.'

'Well, it's here then, Sergeant Brown,' said Mrs Craggs.

The sergeant crouched down to open the cupboard, turning momentarily to Mrs Craggs as he did so and giving her a somewhat baleful look.

'Browne with a "e",' he said creakily, as if he was certain that Mrs Craggs had repeated his name without that final enriching, if mute, letter.

As she had.

Sergeant Browne took one quick look into the cupboard, saw what Mrs Craggs had seen earlier and rose to his feet.

He turned to the other Scotland Yard man, whom Mrs Craggs now swiftly transformed into the detective-superintendent in charge, in spite of his rather undistinguished appearance. He had a snubby button nose and his stripey grey herringbone suit was shiny at the elbows.

'It's murder right enough, guv'nor,' said the sergeant. 'I'll leave the evidence till the team arrives.'

Mrs Craggs did not much like hearing Old Bally Earn Oh

called 'the evidence'. In spite of his infuriating fussiness about such things as the use of House of Lords writing-paper, or rather its misuse, she had liked the old boy and had always woken him as gently as she could on the mornings she had found him curled up in a corner. 'I wonder if he ever comes to in the middle of the night,' Mrs Milhorne had once speculated. 'I wouldn't like to wake and find myself in this creepy old place. Think of what he might of seen.' Ghosts seemed to be in Mrs Milhorne's mind. But Mrs Craggs had not been able to resist saying 'Yeh. Mice, I shouldn't wonder. Amount o' food gets left about.' And Mrs Milhorne had given a delicate breathy shriek.

The detective-superintendent took Sergeant Browne at his word and at once began establishing who the dead man was, accepting Mrs Craggs's temporary identification without demur, despite an attempt by Mr Holofernes to take this important task upon himself.

'Well now, Mrs Craggs,' the superintendent finished, 'I don't think we need keep you any more just now. But if you'd stay in the building, you'd oblige me. I'll want to see you again shortly. My name's Brown, by the way. Brown. Without an "e".'

And he gave Mrs Craggs what looked suspiciously like the merest flick of a wink.

So Mrs Craggs went and waited outside and saw all the bustle. The men Sergeant Browne had referred to as 'the team' arrived, experts every one, carrying bulky boxes and cameras and tripods and a green canvas stretcher and trying not to look overawed by their unusually august surroundings. And the Press arrived and were met full-face by Mr Holofernes, but stopped in front of him only long enough to hear him 'venture to remind you gentlemen of the recent hencounter between Tryulph, fourteenth Earl Balerno and Gosforth, and his Lordship the Bishop of Porchester' before nudging each other crudely in the ribs and sweeping past, eyes intent on the closed door of Committee Room F.

But there they met Sergeant Browne – 'with an "e" if you

please, gentlemen, when you come to file your reports' – and found an altogether more formidable obstacle, though they were eventually promised a statement from Detective-Superintendent Brown – 'without an "e" as it happens, gentlemen' – in about an hour's time.

Mrs Craggs was standing an hour later near the open door of Committee Room G, where the Press conference was held, talking to Mrs Milhorne who had not been asked to stay but thought she should not travel on her own 'after the shock'. So she chanced to hear most of what the button-nosed superintendent said. It was not a great deal, however, mostly about 'an investigation in its very early stages' and having 'reason to believe the case is one of foul play' and 'fullest inquiries' and 'many lines yet to be followed up'. But it was when, after this, she overheard one of the departing reporters, a young man with heavy hornrim spectacles, say: 'Police Baffled, that's what it amounts to, boys', that she decided that she had a duty which she had to perform.

So she knocked on the now closed Committee Room door and when it was opened by Sergeant Browne said she wanted to see the superintendent.

'My good woman,' said the sergeant, 'Detective-Superintendent Brown is a very busy man.'

'I dare say,' said Mrs Craggs. 'But I was the one what found the body, you know. And I've got something as I wants to tell him.'

'I am aware of your role in the affair,' Sergeant Browne replied. 'And I have to inform you that in due course we shall require to take your fingerprints. This will be strictly for elimination purposes, and at the end of the inquiry you will have the right to witness their destruction, if so be you so wish.'

'And when's the end of the inquiry going to be?' Mrs Craggs asked trenchantly.

'That I am unable to say, though I should estimate that, in the nature of things, a period of some weeks should elapse.'

'Would you?' said Mrs Craggs, after she had worked out what all the words meant. 'Some weeks, eh? Well, I should estimate that it'll be in the nature o' some minutes.'

Sergeant Browne sighed.

'If you have information which you believe may contribute to the successful outcome of our inquiry,' he said, and the emphasis he put on 'you believe' would have sunk a smallish battleship, 'then I suggest you impart the same to me without further delay.'

'No,' said Mrs Craggs.

'My good woman, either you have something to tell us, in which case you would do well to tell me immediately, or you have not, in which case I would request you not to take up more of my not unvaluable time.'

'Yeh,' said Mrs Craggs. 'And now can I see the Super?'

'You may not.'

Mrs Craggs considered for an instant.

'All right,' she said, 'I'll tell you this much. It's to do with a suspect.'

Sergeant Browne looked at her, his face solemn with scepticism.

'I suppose it's the Bishop of Porchester,' he said. 'Same as your mate Holofernes, or whatever he calls himself, gave us. Very keen to point to the Bishop was Mr Holofernes. Only as it so happens the Bishop was in church at the material time, in front of a congregation of forty-eight mothers of children about to be confirmed.'

'I dare say,' Mrs Craggs replied unperturbed. 'And I might add that mate of mine old Holofernes is not. In fact —'

She gave Sergeant Browne a shrewdly assessing look.

'In fact, it was Mr Holofernes as I wanted to talk to you about,' she went on. 'Things like a certain taste for House of Lords Madeira wine. Things like a certain habit of old Bally – of the late victim of falling asleep in a corner and maybe waking up in the middle of the night and seeing certain people, whose whole life was in this place, helping themselves to more than what they ought.'

In the lugubrious face in front of her a gleam was slowly entering two mournful brown eyes.

'I thought as how I ought to mention it,' Mrs Craggs continued. 'Specially in view of a certain gentleman what has a dangly gold medallion around his neck being recently seen a-getting into his overcoat.'

'Stay there, my good woman,' said Sergeant Browne, mournful eyes now glowing like two amber traffic lights. 'Stay there and don't move.'

And away he went, almost breaking into an undignified run. But not quite.

And, as soon as his blue-suited back had disappeared round the nearest corner, in went Mrs Craggs to Committee Room G, without so much as knocking.

Detective-Superintendent Brown did not look altogether pleased to see her.

'Mrs Craggs, isn't it?' he said, looking up from the massive copy of *Debrett's Peerage, Baronetage, Knightage and Companionage* which he had been going through with an expression of fair dismay on his button-nosed face. 'I'm afraid I'm rather busy just now, but if you'd care to wait.'

'I think I'd better not,' Mrs Craggs answered. 'You see I got something to tell you, an' I've a feeling that I might be stopped by that sergeant of yours if I don't give it you straight away.'

Detective-Superintendent Brown put a ballpoint as a marker among the many pages of *Debrett*.

'All right,' he said, 'tell me.'

Mrs Craggs drew in a deep breath by way of gathering her thoughts.

'Well,' she said, 'it's him really. Sergeant Browne, with an "e".'

The two sharply curious eyes on either side of the button nose went suddenly hard.

'You're not going to tell me Sergeant Browne murdered his lordship, are you?'

'Good lord, no, sir. I mean, why should he ever? No, it's something else about him. Something silly, really. But important. If you know what I mean.'

'Go on.'

'Well, it's this. When he opened that cupboard next door to see if I was round the bend or something and found there really was a murdered body in there, well, he was a bit busy at that moment a-telling me that Browne was spelt with an "e", and I don't think he noticed something. And o' course by the time all those fellers arrived with their cameras an' all I dare say it'd gorn.'

'What had gone, Mrs Craggs?'

'Why, the smell. The strong, strong smell o' peppermint there was when I first opened the cupboard and then shoved the door back across, what Sergeant Browne later left open. That was what first made me look in there, you know. The peppermint.'

'I see. A strong smell of peppermint. And that tells us something, does it?' Detective-Superintendent Brown's undistinguished face was decidedly thoughtful. 'Or at least it tells you something, I suspect, Mrs Craggs.'

'Nuttall's Mintoes,' said Mrs Craggs. 'That Lord Middlehampton always sucking 'em. Ask anybody. And temper. Terrible. Ask anybody else.'

But the person Detective-Superintendent Brown, without an 'e', asked was the Marquess of Middlehampton himself. And that Lord Temporal said right out, 'Of course I made away with the fellow. Blackguard. He'd stolen something very precious from me. Some Mintoes. Nuttall's Mintoes. The fellow was a disgrace to the House. He had to go. He had to go.'

So they took the Marquess of Middlehampton and put him in another sort of house, not quite so distinguished but an equally permanent institution. And Mrs Craggs soon afterwards gave in her notice to the Staff Superintendent because somehow that old House of Lords was not such a place for funny capers any more.

19

It was some months after the inquest on the murdered
peer, an event which was followed up in sections of the
Press by stories 'from Our Crime Team', incidentally
describing, more or less colourfully, the assistance Mrs
Craggs had given the police. She had begun by then to
work at a different Lord's, the cricket ground rather than
the debating chamber, and Mrs Milhorne, as she
generally did, had gravitated to her side. Just as they
finished work one day Mrs Milhorne started to behave in
a way even odder than usual.

'I shan't be getting on that number 2 bus with you,
dear,' she said. 'I got somewhere else as I must be going
to.'

'Oh, yes? An' where's that, then?'

'Where's that? Where's —'

Mrs Milhorne's normally curds-pale face blushed
suddenly red as the post-box she happened to be standing
next to.

'I – I —' she stammered. 'I ham not at liberty to state.'

'Milhorne ain't in quod again, is he?' Mrs Craggs
demanded, though she knew very well that the gentleman
was enjoying one of his rare periods of home life.

'Certainly not. You don't think the tel – you don't think anybody really respectable would have anythink to do with a lady what had a husband incarceriated, do you?'

'Oh. Off to see someone respectable, are you? I wondered why you was a-wearing that diamanté necklace o' yours, and your diamanté watch what doesn't go.'

'Whoever said I was meeting anybody?'

Mrs Milhorne's post-box appearance returned.

'You did, dear,' Mrs Craggs replied cheerfully. 'But don't tell me about it if you don't want to. I ain't one to pry.'

This last claim was not by any means true. Mrs Craggs has a good deal more than the average share of curiosity. But she reckoned that next day Mrs Milhorne would be bound to tell all. She would not be able to help it.

But in this, for once, Mrs Craggs was wrong. Mrs Milhorne had been so solemnly sworn to secrecy that even her overwhelming wish to impress was kept in check.

*   *   *

Mrs Milhorne?

Yaiss, Yaiss. I'm Mrs Milhorne, actually.

Mrs Milhorne, I hope you don't mind us meeting in a hotel like this, but we do have to maintain maximum security.

Oh, yaiss. Yaiss. I quite understand. Like you said on the phone. Upon the telephone, I should say.

Good. Good. Well, do let's sit down. Would you like a coffee?

No. No. Actually, I've got nerves, you know. Yaiss, nerves.

Tea then?

Oh, yaiss. A nice cuppa – a small pot of tea might be of assistance. In preparing me mind, you know.

Yes. I'll order that, then. Now, shall we begin? I understand you know Mrs Craggs rather well?

Yaiss. Yaiss. I'm her best friend. I think you could say that. On the programme you could say that. The best friend of the participant is Mrs Florence Milhorne.

Well, if we need to …

But – but ain't I – I mean, ham I not to make an appearance? It'd be a strain, of course, a great strain. But in the interests of the television I would be prepared to make the sacrifice.

Well, we don't like to have too many people the Victim sees every day.

Oh. Well, I'm not sure that I —

But – but we'll think about it. Yes, I'm sure my Producer would want to use you, if it's at all possible.

Oh, well then. I mean, I wouldn't like to happear on just any programme. Some of them quizzes – some of those quizzes are very bad taste, if you want my opinion. But 'This Is Your Life' is classy, I always say. Very classy.

I'm glad you think so. Now – ah, here's your tea, and my coffee. Well, shall we get down to it? Did I gather on the phone that you two cleaning ladies have been involved in other cases besides the House of Lords affair?

Ladies what assist, I prefer to say. Mrs Craggs is a lady what assists. And when my 'ealth, my health permits, I assist also.

Ah. I'll try to remember that. Now, can you tell me, for instance, just how old Mrs Craggs is?

How old? I'm sure I've never asked. A lady doesn't. Oh, what have I said? Of course, television's different. Anybody'd be pleased to answer television. I'm in my fifties, actually. Well, mid-fifties. So Mrs Craggs, well, it's difficult to say just what age she is. She doesn't seem to change much, if you know what I mean, always that same old nut-brown face, an' always that same flowered apron and that sort of squashed red hat of hers. An' every time we 'appen – every time we happen to be assisting in the same situation she seems just the same. I suppose she just has to be. So as to sort of, well, triumph when all those things 'appen – happen to her.

I'm not sure I quite understand.

Well, I mean, it's just the same every time, isn't it? Murders and crimes, an' all them funny coincidences. It's funny a lady what assists should come across so many 'orrible deaths an' has so many coincidences 'appen – happen to her. But I suppose unless those sort o' things 'appened to her – well, happened to me as much as her reely – then we wouldn't sort of, well, exist, neither of us, would we?

I – er – suppose not. But, tell me, do you always work with Mrs Craggs?

Yaiss. Yaiss. I do. Well, mostly. It's funny the way we get to be in the same place those times when Mrs Craggs sort of needs somebody to ask questions to her. More like that Dr Watson an' that Sherlock Holmes, what I saw on the telly – upon the television, I should say. He was always asking questions, Dr Watson. Questions that sort of helped the detective to come up with the right answer, to my way of seeing it. An' credit ought to go where credit's due, if there's any justice in the world. I suppose you wouldn't change your minds about which of us you want on the programme?

Well, I don't think we quite ... But I wanted to ask you: how is it she – I mean, you both – how is it you have worked so often in such places, and so many of them?

Well, I don't know, actually, how that came about. It makes what we do more sort of interesting, of course, specially for Americans. I mean, only think, if it should so be that an American 'appened – happened to hear about our doings in one of them – those, one of those crime magazines they have over there, about the way I've been able to sort of guide Mrs Craggs to the solution of so many 'orrible murders, they'd be sort of even more interested if the murder had happened to 'appen in some interesting part of historic old London, wouldn't they?

I suppose so.

Not that the first time Mrs Craggs an' I sort of put the police right we were working in London. No. No, it was in the sort o' place a book writer would call Flinwich, if you get my meaning. The sort o' town that might be anywhere in dear old England. If there chanced to be a theatre there that 'appened, that happened to be used sometimes for opera. An' that's a funny thing, now I come to mention it, Mrs Craggs liking that sort o' music, an' knowing about it. I mean, you'd of expected me, with my feelings, to be the one who'd do that.

II

Mrs Craggs Sings a Different Tune

Mrs Craggs put her duster into her apron pocket and wiped her hands.

'I'm ready,' she said to the detective-sergeant who had summoned her to see Superintendent Pryde, just arrived in Flinwich from Scotland Yard to investigate the death of the young soprano singing the lead role in the never before performed opera *Death of a Fat God*. 'He's in the director's office, isn't he, your Pryde of the Yard?'

The sergeant led the way.

Superintendent Pryde had succeeded in transforming the office. It was not clear to Mrs Craggs at first exactly what he had done. But it no longer looked like the showplace of an advanced airline. It had a more homely, more squalid look.

The big abstract canvases still hung from the walls but next to the most striking of them, Mrs Craggs realised, the superintendent had hung from a fitting at the top of the window his well-used macintosh. And on the smart ebony desk he had plonked down a battered briefcase, a plate of sandwiches and two bottles of beer.

Mrs Craggs looked at the food and drink sternly.

The superintendent appeared to guess what she was thinking.

'I'm sorry I've made such a mess,' he said. 'Perhaps in fact you'd be kind enough to deal with it when we've had our little talk.'

He smiled broadly.

'The fact of the matter is,' he said, 'that I didn't get any lunch. I had a meeting and it lasted longer than I expected. The Press, you know. So I got hold of a little light refreshment afterwards.'

'Very natural, I'm sure.'

The superintendent looked at her.

'Well, now,' he said, 'let's get down to business for the present. Would you be good enough to take a seat?'

He gestured towards the elegant Swedish chair which he had set facing the desk at an uncompromising angle.

Mrs Craggs sat on the edge of it.

The superintendent opened a buff file in front of him and began slowly reading the single slip of paper it contained.

Mrs Craggs was not going to put up with this.

'I hear from Mr Strutt, the stage-door keeper, that you're satisfied there were only eleven of us in the whole building at the time of the murder,' she said.

'Well,' he said, 'I can see I shan't have to beat about the bush with you, Mrs Craggs. Yes, subject to further inquiries, you can take it that there were eleven people only here at the time in question.'

'Then you shouldn't have much difficulty, should you?'

Superintendent Pryde shifted in his chair.

'Let me tell you,' he said, 'that that's by no means the case. It isn't often you have a murder committed and find eleven people each of whom could have done it without being seen by any of the others.'

The look of surprise on Mrs Craggs's face seemed to please him. He relaxed in his chair again.

'Yes,' he went on, 'unless you're going to tell me that you were able to see any of the eleven without them seeing you, that is precisely the situation that confronts me.'

He sounded as if he was some gourmet facing a large, rare and appetising dish.

He tilted his chair back.

'It's quite extraordinary really,' he said. 'You get a comparatively small area such as the stage of this theatre, and you have eleven people there. But it so happens that at a certain point in time, i.e., at the instant the weights were taken off that god's car contrivance and that girl was crushed by the balancing platform on the inside of the scenery, not one of those eleven people was with another of them.'

'Not young Albert Sime what was up in what they calls the fly gallery waiting to operate the brakes on that god's car thing?' Mrs Craggs asked.

'Him! I don't think I've ever had the pleasure of dealing with a less useful witness.'

The superintendent glanced up at Sergeant Jenkins for confirmation. The sergeant was prompt to nod agreement.

'Not only did the stupid lad faint as soon as he saw the ropes flying through the brake blocks,' Superintendent Pryde said, 'but he spent the whole time he was up in the gallery staring at the levers to make sure he would release the right ones when the time came.'

'They ought never to have left him there all by himself,' said Mrs Craggs. 'He's only a boy.'

'Well, that's as may be, but the fact remains that he was completely unhelpful to me. Any one of ten people – eleven if you count Sime himself – could have got at those weights.'

He looked straight at Mrs Craggs.

'You could have done,' he said.

Mrs Craggs said nothing.

With slow menace the superintendent turned over the piece of paper in the open buff file. And, finding Mrs Craggs gazing at it with calm curiosity, looked down himself and saw its back was entirely blank.

'Look, Mrs Craggs,' he said, 'I've already had occasion to remark that you appear to be a woman of keen observation. You notice things.'

He paused and looked up into the air above her head.

'I suppose it comes from your job,' he said. 'If your duty is to clear up any messes that are made, then you keep an eye out for things.'

He leant forward and looked at her directly.

'However,' he said, 'that is by the way. The point is: have you seen or heard anything in the past few days, either before the murder or after it, that you think might have a bearing on the matter?'

'I can't say that I have.'

'No? Well, I didn't expect you to be able to answer yes. After all, you haven't got a mind trained to know what might or might not be relevant to an affair like this. So I want to put a different question to you.'

The large eyes boring into her.

'I want to put this question: have you at any time in the recent past noticed anything unusual, anything at all, about any of the ten other people in the theatre when this business happened?'

Mrs Craggs did not answer until she had had a good think.

'No,' she replied at last. 'No, I can't say I have.'

'Nothing whatsoever?'

'Nothing.'

'Nothing, no matter how trivial or silly?'

'I said nothing.'

The superintendent leant back in his chair.

'Well,' he said, 'let's go about it in another way.'

He picked up a pencil and twiddled it.

'For instance,' he said, 'when Sergeant Jenkins here asked you to come and see me, what were you doing? Where were you at that very moment?'

'I was working. I was in Herr Prahler's dressing-room.'

'I see. Now, did you notice anything out of the ordinary there? Anything at all not quite as you're used to seeing it?'

'Are you suggesting that I go prying round when I'm at work in the dressing-rooms?'

The superintendent smiled.

'No, no. Not one bit. Though, mind you, I wouldn't blame you if you did. What's the harm in it? What's the harm in a little natural curiosity?'

'Plenty, if the person you're being curious about happens to be in the room at the time.'

'Oh. Oh, I see. Herr Prahler was there, was he?'

'He was.'

'And you talked to him?'

'He talked to me.'

'What about?'

'What do you think? He talked about the murder, of course. When a thing like that happens you stop talking about the weather. You've something worth discussing at last. And in any case it's worrying for him. That girl meant a lot to him as a pupil. For his future, like.'

'Very good. He said that, did he?'

'More or less.'

'Excellent. And what else did he say? As far as you're able to remember, of course.'

'He didn't say all that much. Only that the poor girl was a hard worker and didn't have many friends over here.'

'That we already know.'

'You asked me what he said and I'm telling you.'

'Quite right, quite right. You just go on telling me. Don't let what you think might or might not be important make any difference. You just tell me everything.'

'All right. Well, he said it was a terrible pity her being killed because now no one would ever know what a good teacher he was. He thought it'd be too late or something. Then he went on to wonder why anyone should kill her at all.'

'I don't blame him. So do I. And what then?'

'Nothing.'

'Nothing?'

'Yes, I was just making some sort of remark like in answer and your Sergeant Jenkins knocked at the door.'

'I see.'

Superintendent Pryde tapped six or seven times with the butt end of the pencil on the surface of the ebony desk.

He sighed.

'What were you saying to him?'

'Just that it looked to me as if the girl wasn't meant to be killed at all.'

The black jutting eyebrows shot together.

'That it was really meant to be Monsieur Pivoine, you know,' Mrs Craggs explained. 'Him what so many of 'em have had rows with an' that. Him as is a real nasty if ever I met one.'

'I see.'

Superintendent Pryde stood up.

'Well,' he said, 'I think that will be all.'

Mrs Craggs got up and took the dirty plate and the empty beer-bottles off the desk.

'By the way,' the superintendent said, 'I wouldn't go mentioning that notion of yours to too many people. Might get you into trouble, you know. It's not very likely, really.'

'I never said it was,' Mrs Craggs replied. 'I only told you what I said to Herr Prahler. You asked me, you know. We were just going over what happened, the way people do. It was my turn to say something, and so that's what I said.'

The superintendent nodded.

'Oh, yes,' he said. 'There's no reason why you shouldn't have made the remark. But I thought I ought to draw your attention to the fact that it's the sort of thing that makes for bad feeling. It would make people think a whole lot of people had got reasons for being a murderer. I dare say you hadn't thought of that aspect. Good day.'

In the corridor outside Mrs Craggs saw Mrs Milhorne.

'Hallo, dear,' she said. 'I missed you when I came back dinner time.'

'Yaiss,' said Mrs Milhorne, 'I came all over queer when I was having dinner and I had to have a bit of a lay-down before I came back.'

'You all right now, dear?'

'Yes, thank you, dear. Not too bad, that is. Of course, it all started up again the moment I arrived. I still feel fluttery when I think of it.'

'What of?'

'Of it. Of that Pryde of the Yard.'

'Oh. You been to see him, too, have you, dear?'

'Yes. No sooner was I back when he sent for me. That's why I was waiting for you when you came out. I thought you might be feeling like me.'

'I'm feeling all right,' said Mrs Craggs.

'Well, I dare say you didn't have the time of it I did. And then I've got what I call a sensitive nature.'

'So I've heard you say.'

'So you can't wonder that it made me feel not too good, can you?'

'I don't see why it should have done. He couldn't eat you.'

'No, but it was the strain. You didn't have that. That's what makes the difference. Especially to someone like me.'

'What strain?'

'The strain of not telling, of course.'

'Not telling? What have you got not to tell, I should like to know.'

'What I heard. I couldn't tell him that, could I? I couldn't tell him all that.'

Mrs Craggs looked at Mrs Milhorne. Unbendingly.

'When I was in there just now,' she said, 'he asked me whether I had heard or seen anything that might have a bearing on this business. Did he ask you the same?'

'Oh, yaiss,' said Mrs Milhorne. 'That was the worst moment really. I thought I should faint.'

'And you didn't tell him about whatever it is you heard?'

Mrs Milhorne bridled.

'Of course I didn't,' she said. 'I keep telling you, don't I? It was all I could do not to show it on my face. That's the trouble with feeling things so deep: they show.'

'And all this has definitely got something to do with Mary Arthur and her being killed?'

'Of course it has. It was her, don't you realise that? It was her I couldn't help overhearing. That was what made it so dreadful.'

'And what exactly did you listen to her saying? And who was she saying it to?'

Mrs Craggs did not attempt to conceal her curiosity.

'But to Jean-Artaban Pivoine.'

A certain delicacy of feeling forbade Mrs Milhorne adding 'Who else could it be?'

'So you heard Jean-Artaban and Mary Arthur saying something? Something that showed there was something between them, or what?'

'It wasn't Jean-Artaban I heard so much. It was her. Though I could see he was there. They were standing just inside the scene dock. I suppose to get a bit of privacy. But, of course, there's no door there, though it is out of the way. So if anyone was near enough they could hear everything that was being said.'

'It was Mary Arthur who was doing the speaking, was it?'

'It certainly was. And using language, too. I didn't never think a lady would use language quite like that.'

'Mary Arthur was a nice kid, but she was no lady.'

'Well,' said Mrs Milhorne, 'perhaps it was her being Australian. Because you can't tell me she wasn't a lady, underneath. She was a singer.'

'You're a singer because you've got a voice. It doesn't make any difference to the sort of person you are.'

'Well, I don't believe that.'

'It's just a matter of having been born with vocal chords a tiny bit different from everyone else's and a slightly different shape inside your 'ead.'

'I don't think that's at all nice, dear. I tell you straight I don't.'

'Never mind whether it's nice or not, my girl. It's the truth. But what I want to know is: what was Mary Arthur saying to Jean-Artaban?'

Mrs Milhorne looked away.

'Come on, now, I want to hear. You've told me she was saying something pretty strong and I mean to get to know what it was if I have to go on badgering you all day to get it out of you.'

'Well, reely.'

'Yes, really.'

'Well, I suppose I'll have to tell you, then. Though I'm not sure that I should.'

A faint, irregular blush showed on Mrs Milhorne's sallow cheeks.

'Well, you know what Jean-Artaban's like, don't you?' she said.

'I know very well what he's like. He's like a devil most of the time. But which sort of a devil was he being this time?'

'It's difficult for me to say.'

'Then you'll have to make your mind up to it. You heard this row, you can't keep it secret now.'

Mrs Milhorne sighed.

'I suppose I can't really.'

'No, you can't. What was it he was after? Come on, out with it.'

Mrs Milhorne came out with it.

'Sex,' she said.

'I guessed as much,' said Mrs Craggs. 'And she wasn't as willing as he'd thought she'd be?'

Mrs Milhorne's blush deepened.

'Something like that,' she said.

Mrs Craggs turned towards the door of the director's office.

'And now,' she said, 'you're going to repeat all that to the superintendent.'

'What, me?'

'Yes, you.'

'But I couldn't. I mean not to him. Not to Pryde of the Yard. Not all that.'

'Why not?'

Mrs Milhorne looked down at her shoes. They had a twirling pattern of little punched holes.

'Well,' she said, 'it's him being him, like, you know, Pryde of the Yard. Famous. Somehow I couldn't bring myself to talk about a thing like that with a famous man. I just couldn't.'

'Listen,' said Mrs Craggs, 'he's a policeman, isn't he? He knows that men make passes at girls.'

'Oh, I know that. I know that. Look at the Bedhampton Strangler case that he pulled off so well. He'd have had to have known some pretty seamy facts of life for that. But it's somehow me talking to him about them that I can't imagine. It'd be like asking a film star if you could use their toilet.'

'Well,' said Mrs Craggs, 'if it's any help to you I can't see that the Bedhampton case makes him such a great man, for all the papers went on and on about it so. After all, the man was mad. Anyone could see that. He thought he was God Almighty. It should have been easy enough to spot him.'

Mrs Milhorne shook her head.

'I don't know about that,' she said.

'Well,' said Mrs Craggs, 'I do know about this. Pryde of the Yard or no Pryde of the Yard, he'll want to know what you've just told me and you're going straight in there to tell him.'

And she opened the door and gave Mrs Milhorne a slight but firm shove.

Mrs Milhorne turned round for a moment as if she would rush back out. But Mrs Craggs heard Superintendent Pryde pounce on her and ask her by name if he could help.

'Well, I don't know,' she heard Mrs Milhorne reply.

The simper in her voice was enough. Mrs Craggs sharply shut the door.

Mrs Milhorne was in with the superintendent for only three minutes.

When she came out Mrs Craggs was waiting for her.

Mrs Milhorne looked crestfallen.

'He didn't seem interested, reely,' she said.

'Not interested? You're sure?'

'Yes, and I can see why, too.'

'Oh, why?'

'It was something he said to that nice Sergeant Jenkins.'

'What did he say?'

'Something about the boot being on the other foot. Do you know what, dear? I think he's found out that the person who did it wasn't trying to kill Mary Arthur at all. They were trying to kill Jean-Artaban.'

36

Yes. Yes, that's very interesting. I'll have to run down to – what did you say the place was called? – Flinwich, and see —

Yaiss. It is funny old Elma Craggs should know all about operas called *Death of A Fat God* an' such, let alone the way in the end she knew just who'd killed that girl on the stage and 'appened – happened to beat Pryde of the Yard to the solution.

Did she do that? Really? I must say, reading up the case in the files, I got the impression it was Pryde of the Yard who solved it so brilliantly.

Yaiss, you would of, of course. Elma Craggs don't seem to like to take the credit, you know. Just like that Sherlock Holmes I saw on the telly – I beg yours, upon the television. But, yaiss, it was Elma who, when Pryde of the Yard wanted to arrest Jean-Artaban's former wife, just stopped him in time and showed him who the real killer was.

Yes, the man who was —

Stop. Stop.

Stop?

Well, if all that was one o' them whodunits, you wouldn't want anybody who hadn't read the book to know, would you? And it was more like something that had happened in a book than real life, that was.

Yes. But, tell me, Mrs Milhorne, you and Mrs Craggs have almost always worked together, haven't you? Even in the days when you were in — er — Flinwich?

Oh, yaiss. Yaiss. We worked — assisted a good many different parties there, one way and another. I mean, if we ain't of done, that is, if we had not never, Mrs Craggs would not have hencountered so many murderers, would she?

No, I suppose not. And she hen — encountered other criminals besides murderers, did she, in those early days?

Oh, yaiss. Otherwise her hencounters would have been a bit what I call samey, wouldn't they. Still, it was funny, reely, how five things should hoccur to her that sort of demonstrated her five senses. You'd think it'd been arranged somehow, wouldn't you?

III

THE FIVE SENSES OF MRS CRAGGS
SEEING

OF ALL THE VARIOUS CLEANING jobs that Mrs Craggs had in her earlier days, the one at the place they called Murray's House was the one she liked best. Yet she was the person most responsible, when you came down to it, for bringing that job to an end.

Murray's House had belonged in the eighteenth century to old Peter Murray, the inventor and discoverer and gatherer of curiosities, and eventually it had been left to the borough, which kept it as nearly as possible the way it had been and charged the public to see it. Not that many of the public were willing to pay, but there it was.

Certainly Mrs Craggs got to like the old place very much. It used to please her to think, when she toiled up the stairs, that she was seeing exactly the same twirls and curls in the banisters that old Peter Murray had seen all those years before. And though she did not particularly understand many of the curious wooden machines and other things the house was filled with, she liked them all the same. Old Peter Murray had worked on them and put his skill and care into them, and you could tell.

So it was all the more terrible when Mrs Craggs arrived for work one morning with Mrs Milhorne and found that the night porter, old Mr Berbottle, had been murdered, an event which was to result before too long in the final closing of the old House. Thanks to Mrs Craggs.

Of course everybody said at once that there could be no doubt who had killed Mr Berbottle: the skinheads of those days. They were always breaking into places, and this time poor crotchety, pernickety old Mr Berbottle must have disturbed them and for that had had his head laid open with a piece of lead piping. And all the previous day's receipts, such as they were, had disappeared.

The worst of it was that this had been the first time the money had been left on the premises overnight. Generally, after the manager, Mr Fingles, had checked it, the money was taken and put in the night safe of the bank by Mr Tanker, the day porter, a rippling-muscled former bosun of a sail-training ship, who stood no nonsense from skinheads or anyone else. But Mr Tanker had been taken ill at lunchtime, and the manager had said there would be no harm in leaving the money in the house for just one night. He and Mr Berbottle between them were quite capable of looking after it. Only, when it had come to it, Mr Fingles, who was notorious for liking his half-bottle of rather fine wine with his dinner, had been so soundly asleep in his comfortable little private flat at the top of the house that he had not heard a thing.

So there the police were all over the place and there was little Mr Fingles, who had discovered the body when he had come down to collect the post, in more of a state of agitation than usual, rushing up and down on his little clickety heels and getting in everybody's way. 'Like a regular old clockwork doll,' Mrs Craggs had murmured to Mrs Milhorne as they waited for the fingerprint men and the police photographer and all the rest to finish.

They had a long wait of it too, with nothing more exciting to see for most of the time than the detective-superintendent in charge prowling about and looking important, though, as Mrs Milhorne said, 'It isn't as if it's exactly what you'd call a mystery killing, is it?' But at last the superintendent himself came up to the two of them.

'Very well, ladies,' he said, 'I shall be here for some time to come, I expect, but there's nothing to stop you two going ahead with your work now. My lads have got everything they want.'

And then he paused and became a bit uneasy. 'There is one thing, though,' he added. 'The porter's room there, where it happened.'

'Yes?' said Mrs Craggs, glancing along to the little room with the ticket window.

'Well,' said the superintendent, still looking uncomfortable, 'the fact of the matter is there's – well, there's what you might call traces on the floor in there, and I don't know whether you'd object to – er – dealing with them.'

'I couldn't,' declared Mrs Milhorne, with great promptness. 'I'm afraid to say I'd come all over queer. I'd be bound to. I've got nerves, you see.'

'You don't have to do it,' Mrs Craggs broke in. 'The porter's room's got lino on the floor, and lino polishing's my department, always has been.'

She turned to the superintendent and jerked her head at Mrs Milhorne. 'She's dusting,' she said.

So off to her dusting went Mrs Milhorne, though not without putting a hand to her skinny chest and declaring she could 'feel the heartbeats something terrible'. And Mrs Craggs matter-of-factly fetched herself a pail of hot water and a scrubbing brush and tackled the porter's room, thinking all the while how old Mr Berbottle had been so nosy and pernickety and interfering, and how now none of it had done him any good.

It was only later, when she was on her knees polishing the thin strip of brown linoleum that edged the entrance hall, that she came across something that made her stop suddenly and rise to her feet with a decidedly grim expression on her face.

'Mrs Milhorne, dear,' she called to her friend, who was half-way up the stairs, busy doing some fancywork with her duster on the twirls and twiddles of the old banisters.

'Yes, dear?'

'I think I'm just going to have a word with that

superintendent. I want to tell him about this footprint on the lino.'

'Footprint on the lino?'

Mrs Milhorne abandoned her dusting and came down to look. She found her friend standing with sturdy legs wide apart over a footprint, or to be accurate half a footprint, just on the edge of the lino where it met the broad, but very threadbare, central carpet.

'It's a bare foot,' Mrs Milhorne pronounced after a long inspection. 'Looking as if it was on its way to go out by the front door.'

'Yes, dear,' said Mrs Craggs.

'And you're going to the superintendent about it? Well, I know you don't like to have your polish trod on when you've just got it looking all nice, but to go to Scotland Yard about that – well, it beats all.'

And Mrs Milhorne indulged in her favourite trilling laugh.

'He's not Scotland Yard, he's local,' said Mrs Craggs, and off she stumped.

Mrs Milhorne decided to have a rest from her dusting and stay where she was by the footprint. To her immense surprise scarcely ten minutes later Mrs Craggs came back with the superintendent, and the great man himself actually squatted down and closely examined the half-footprint. Then he pushed himself to his feet and set off up the stairs, looking extremely thoughtful.

At the turn, however, he encountered the manager, coming click-clacking excitedly down. And it was then that Mrs Milhorne got her biggest surprise of all.

'Mr Fingles,' the superintendent said in a voice doom-laden with formality. 'I should like you to accompany me to the station, where I have a number of questions I wish to put to you.'

It was not until it was in the paper that Mr Fingles had been charged with the murder that Mrs Craggs agreed to answer a single one of the many questions Mrs Milhorne had plagued her with. Then she did explain.

'Clear as the nose on me face really, dear, when you come to think,' she said. 'Why would a naked footprint be right here on the lino at the edge of the hall?'

'I'm sure I don't know,' Mrs Milhorne replied. 'Unless someone just happened to be creeping along there.'

'Of course they were creeping, dear. And who would have to creep specially quiet so as to get right up close to old Mr Berbottle if it wasn't someone he knew and would wonder what they were doing carrying a piece of lead piping? Especially if it was someone who can't walk about anywhere without making a noise like a little old tip-tapping clockwork doll?'

Mrs Milhorne pondered over this at length.

'I suppose you're right, dear,' she said at last. 'But I would've thought a bare footprint like that meant our Mr Tanker, not Mr Fingles. Mr Tanker was always saying how he wore no shoes when he went climbing up all those masts on that ship of his.'

'And why would Mr Tanker want to murder Mr Berbottle?' Mrs Craggs demanded.

'I'm sure I don't know, dear. But, come to that, why did Mr Fingles want to murder him?'

'Because of the money, of course,' Mrs Craggs answered. 'And Mr Fingles with his nice bottles of wine to buy and his flat up there what he's made so comfortable.'

'The money?' Mrs Milhorne asked.

'Yes, the money. Wasn't this the first time the money had been left here overnight? And wasn't Mr Berbottle, rest him, just the sort of interfering old fool who would go and check it against the tickets issued, even though he knew that was Mr Fingles's job?'

It took Mrs Milhorne a little time to sort it all out, but she got there in the end.

'You mean Mr Fingles had been pinching a bit of the takings all along, to help him out, like?' she said. 'Now, why couldn't I of seen that?'

Mrs Craggs gave her a slow smile.

'Because you ain't very keen to get down on your 'ands and knees, dear,' she said, 'and see what's in front of your face.'

THE FIVE SENSES OF MRS CRAGGS
SMELLING

WHEN MRS CRAGGS HAD THE the washing-up job at a select residential hotel on the outskirts of a town that might be called Flinwich, she used to allow herself a little treat in the summertime. Between finishing the lunch dishes and beginning on the tea things she took a cup for herself and sat with it in the storeroom. It was not exactly comfortable. Mrs Craggs had to perch herself on a packing case and there was very little light.

But it had one distinct advantage as far as Mrs Craggs was concerned: a row of frosted-glass louvre windows high up in the wall that formed the back of the hotel's delightful rose garden. So, in consequence, Mrs Craggs, sitting on that packing case in the gloom of the storeroom amid a strong smell of soap, was often able to hear the most fascinating conversations.

She was quite unashamed of this. As she said to Mrs Milhorne, to whom she retailed certain, but not all, of the things she heard, 'If they don't know I'm listening, then it don't do them no harm. And I think it's interesting.' And so, day by day, she contrived to get a notion of almost all the hotel's regular guests, and even visitors who came only for tea could sometimes be added to her bag.

So when, one day, sitting on her accustomed uncomfortable seat, she heard old Mr Danchflower refer to the elderly visitor with whom he was taking tea as 'Lady Etherege', Mrs Craggs pricked up her ears. Mrs Milhorne enjoyed feeling she was getting a worm's-eye view of the aristocracy and it did no harm to have a titbit to feed to Mrs Milhorne from time to time.

Not that, it soon developed, Lady Etherege was any great shakes when you came down to it. She was blue-blooded all right – you could tell that just by listening to her delicate, tired old voice – but she was far from being rich. Of course, she had not come right out with that. Not when it was probably the first time she had met old Mr Danchflower who, though he might not be particularly aristocratic, was certainly well off, as you had to be to stay in one of the hotel's best rooms summer and winter alike.

Yet, bit by bit, as Mrs Craggs savoured her good, big, strong cup of tea and listened to the two elderly voices floating in through the louvre above her, it became quite plain that old Lady Etherege lived like a church mouse.

Mrs Craggs began to feel really sorry for her. It was all right being poor when you were used to it, but to end your days like that when you'd begun grand as grand, that was hard. Not that Lady Etherege did not have compensations, it seemed. She even had, so her conversation revealed little by little, an admirer.

Admittedly he was an admirer at a distance. Over in France. And the form his admiration took was no more than sending her for each birthday a bottle of perfume. But what perfume! Mrs Craggs gathered that the latest bottle had actually been taken, with great reverence, out of Lady Etherege's handbag and that now its stopper was being gently removed and Mr Danchflower was being permitted a discreet inhalation.

'Oh, excellent,' Mrs Craggs heard him say. 'Really, madam, a most delicate scent. What shall I say it reminds me of? Not these roses even. It's far more subtle than that.'

'Yes, yes,' came Lady Etherege's voice. 'It comes from a past age. An age I once knew, let me admit it.'

Mrs Craggs could have sworn she even heard the sigh through the narrow slits of the frosted-glass louvre.

'Ah,' Lady Etherege added, 'there was a time, my dear sir, when I myself had no hesitation in entering a boutique in the Rue St Honoré and buying perfume at twenty-five pounds for a tiny bottle.'

'Twenty-five pounds,' said old Mr Danchflower. 'I can well believe this cost that much, madam. A most remarkably fine and delicate scent.'

'Oh, well,' Lady Etherege answered, her simper, too, almost floating through the narrow window, 'since we are friends I can tell you that this tiny bottle actually cost even more than that. My dear, dear old admirer accidentally left the bill in the parcel last year and before I crumpled it up I could not help noticing that the sum mentioned was the equivalent – you'll hardly believe this, but everything is so very very expensive nowadays – was the equivalent of no less than forty pounds.'

'Indeed, indeed, madam. But I do believe it I assure —'

And then through the open louvre came what could only be described as a feminine shriek of utter horror, followed an instant later by the small but unmistakable sound of breaking glass.

'Madam, how could I? – I – I don't know what I did. I could have sworn the bottle was safe on the arm of the bench, but ...'

Old Mr Danchflower's voice faded into utterly overwhelmed silence. But, rooted on her packing case, Mrs Craggs could hear all too clearly Lady Etherege's choked sobs, though it was plain she was doing all in her power to restrain them.

And then, seconds later, she heard her own name being loudly called out in the kitchen.

'Mrs Craggs, Mrs Craggs! Where is the woman?'

It was Mr Wipsley, the under-manager, in even more of a tizzy than usual. Mrs Craggs slipped down off the packing case, put down her teacup where it wouldn't be noticed, and emerged.

'Ah, there you are. There you are. Quick, quick, Mrs Craggs, out into the rose garden with a bucket and a cloth. As fast as

you can, as fast as you can. There has been the most terrible
disaster.'

Mrs Craggs, without saying she well knew what the disaster
was, filled a bucket with water, took a floor cloth, and went
round after scuttling Mr Wipsley.

'It's perfume,' Mr Wipsley explained, quite unnecessarily
since the whole of the garden was now smelling to heaven of a
scent that certainly was not that of roses. 'A most unfortunate
accident. But we must sweep it all away on the instant. It must
be as if it had never been.'

So Mrs Craggs scarcely looked at the two sad spectators of
the tragic scene, Mr Danchflower standing erect and still deeply
blushing and little Lady Etherege beside him, dabbing the
daintiest of handkerchiefs to her old tired eyes. Instead Mrs
Craggs swooshed most of the contents of her bucket over the
thick oily stain on the flagstones and then began to mop up till
the pail itself smelled like an oversize bouquet of every flower
you could think of.

And, as she worked, Mrs Craggs heard the two old people
talk.

'Madam, may I say again that I cannot think how I could
have been so abominably careless. I didn't see the bottle, but I
suppose my sleeve must have just caught it.'

'It's perfectly all right.'

'No. No, madam, it is not all right. You have lost something
extremely valuable to you, not only financially but
sentimentally. It is not all right, madam.'

'It – it was of some sentimental value, yes.'

'Madam, that I can never repair. But at least – please be so
good as to let me write you a cheque for forty pounds.'

'Oh, no. No, really. Really I could not.'

But old Mr Danchflower had sat down on the bench, taken
out his chequebook, and was already writing. Lady Etherege
sat down beside him.

'No, really, sir,' she said. 'From an acquaintance of such
short standing I could not possibly —'

'Nonsense, madam, nonsense. There, take it!'

'Well. Well, if you insist … And there I do believe I see the stopper left in the neck of the bottle. I think I will just keep it. You know, a – a souvenir.'

Her frail old hand reached down to somewhere near where Mrs Craggs's floor cloth was at work and the fingers closed round the ornate glass. And then Mrs Craggs's fingers closed round Lady Etherege's.

'Oh, no, you don't,' Mrs Craggs said loudly.

'Don't? Don't? I do not understand.'

Beneath Mrs Craggs's grasp the thin fingers wriggled hard.

'Oh, yes, you do,' said Mrs Craggs. 'You understand quite well that this neck's got a false compartment in its top. A compartment filled with the delicate scent Mr Danchflower liked so much, and not with this nasty cheap muck ponging to high heaven.'

And then old Lady Etherege dropped the stopper, slid her hand from Mrs Craggs's grasp, rose in an instant, seized the half-full bucket, emptied its contents all over Mrs Craggs, and was out of the garden, into the street, and had hopped onto a passing bus before anybody else had time to realise what she had done.

And, as Mrs Craggs said, 'For hours and hours afterwards you could tell I was coming round the corner yards before I got there. What a niff!'

THE FIVE SENSES OF MRS CRAGGS
HEARING

W**HEN** M**RS** C**RAGGS** **FIRST WENT** to work for Mrs Proost she
rather liked listening to the old lady's music boxes. They were
her most cherished possession, left to her by her husband, the
Flinwich postmaster, who had died years before and who had
devoted all his spare time to their collection. But, as time
passed and Mrs Proost insisted on playing one box or another
all the while Mrs Craggs was cleaning in the house, she began,
as she said to Mrs Milhorne, 'to really hate the blessed things.'

'I like a good tune,' she said, 'same as anyone else. But to
hear that tinkle, tinkle, tinkle all day and every, why, it's more
than human ears can stand.' Mrs Milhorne wondered how the
old lady herself could put up with it. 'I'll tell you,' said Mrs
Craggs. 'It's because she doesn't hear a single note.'

Why ever not, Mrs Milhorne wanted to know. It wasn't as if
the old lady was deaf, because she'd seen her herself, out doing
a bit of shopping and talking with the best, 'and never a sign of
them little things behind your ear'.

Mrs Craggs had smiled at that. 'Oh,' she said, 'she wouldn't
let on. Go to any lengths she would to pretend she's heard
every word. Nod and smile like an old teetotum. But I know. I
can go into that sitting room of hers and so long as I take good
care to stand where she can't see me lips, I can say, "Wotcher,

me old mate, how's all the little tinkle boxes then?'' and she don't take one blind bit of notice.'

But Mrs Craggs put up with the tinkle-tinkling because Mrs Proost was a nice old thing, even if she was too proud to admit how little she could hear. And all went well. Till the day the old lady asked Mrs Craggs if, as a special favour, she could come back the next afternoon and serve tea.

'It's my nephew,' she said. 'My husband's brother's boy. Tony. Such a dear little fellow he used to be, though I'm afraid his parents, poor dear souls, spoiled him dreadfully.'

Mrs Craggs replied that certainly she would come the next day at three and she asked how it was that the young man had never visited his aunt in all the time she had been working for her.

'Oh, but you see,' said Mrs Proost, 'he's been dreadfully busy. Yes, in the North. He's been away in the North for – oh, for quite eight years now. A most important post.'

'What's that then?' asked Mrs Craggs, using her lips hard.

'Oh, dear. Well, you will think me silly, but I can't quite recall. It was something to do with aeroplanes, I think. Or was it aerodromes? But it was important. I can tell you that.'

*　*　*

Mrs Craggs had been in the kitchen, slicing bread nice and thin, for some twenty minutes when the visitor arrived. She answered his ring at the door and showed him into the sitting room. But she was not impressed. Nephew Tony was a good deal older than Mrs Proost had led her to expect, and he had too travel-worn a look for someone with an important job to do with aeroplanes, or even airports. As he walked ahead of her across the hall, she thought she could hear one of the soles of shoes flapping slightly, and certainly both shoes were covered with a fine layer of dust.

So, instead of retiring discreetly until four o'clock, when it had been agreed she should bring in tea, Mrs Craggs contrived to stand by the door of the room, as if she was, despite her flowered apron and best hat worn in honour of the event, a sort of footman.

Nephew Tony was very breezy and bold, and Mrs Craggs could see old Mrs Proost looking at his face carefully as he sat opposite her and so succeeding in answering his hearty remarks about thinking he 'wouldn't bother with a taxi from the station, just gave myself a tuppenny bus ride, you know.' More like it he walked, thought Mrs Craggs, even though it was three miles.

But just then Mrs Proost realised that the charwoman was still hovering over the proceedings.

'Mrs Craggs,' she said, 'you may serve tea.'

'Bit early, ain't it?' Mrs Craggs asked, after advancing to where her lips could be read.

'Never mind,' Mrs Proost replied, with a dignity recalling the days when she'd had a real maid, in black dress and lace cap. 'Master Tony and I will take tea now.'

'Very good,' said Mrs Craggs. And so impressed was she with the high tone that her employer had achieved, she added, though rather belatedly, 'Madam.'

But nevertheless, out in the kitchen she got the rest of the tea things on to the tray in record time and made the tea itself – in the silver teapot, appearing especially for the occasion – without actually waiting for the pot to warm. And when she entered the sitting room again, she thought she had arrived only just in time.

Nephew Tony was talking about Mrs Proost's music boxes. And what he was saying sent columns of red anger marching through Mrs Craggs's head.

'You see, Aunt,' he was arguing, 'these boxes may be quite valuable and since the truth of it is that, though you play them often enough, you can't really —'

With a fierce jerk of the tea tray between her outstretched arms Mrs Craggs sent a stream of hot liquid from the spout of the silver pot plummeting straight down on to Nephew Tony's lap.

'Oh, lor, sir, lor,' Mrs Craggs said in instant apology. 'What must have come over me? Oh, sir. Sir, you are a mess. Come out to the kitchen right away and I'll sponge you down. We gotter save that nice suit.'

And, though the suit in fact was of a cut and colour that indicated years of service that had begun a long time ago, Nephew Tony did hurry out to the kitchen.

There Mrs Craggs did nothing at all about sponging the broad spatter of tea. Instead she faced the not so young man with her arms akimbo.

'Now you just listen to me,' she said. 'I know what you were just going to tell her. And you're not to do it.'

'What – what do you mean?' Nephew Tony asked.

'I mean you were going to tell her she's so deaf she can't hear the musical boxes. And I daresay you were going to offer to sell 'em for her. And with a big difference between the price you get and the money you'll give her.'

'I don't know what you're talking about,' Nephew Tony said. 'If I was offering my aunt some good business advice, it's hardly any affair of yours. The money she gets for those boxes would probably be enough to keep her in comfort for the rest of her days.'

'She's happy enough as she is, and don't you think nothing else,' Mrs Craggs answered. 'She may not hear a single tinkle those blessed boxes make, but she thinks we all believe she does and that's what keeps her going. So don't you try putting your oar in.'

Nephew Tony, dabbing for himself at his trousers with a snatched dishcloth, darted Mrs Craggs a glance of fury.

'I'll thank you to keep your interfering nose out of our family business,' he said. 'I'm going straight back in there and tell my aunt it's plain common sense to sell those boxes, and that I know where I can get a fair price for them.'

Mrs Craggs folded her hands and stood with them in front of her, leaving the way to the kitchen door clear. But there was a look in her eyes that stopped Nephew Tony dead in his tracks.

'What are you looking like that for?' he blustered.

'Because,' said Mrs Craggs, 'if you go in there I shall come after you and tell your dear aunt that her nephew's just finished a good spell in quod.'

'Prison? How did you know – what do you mean, "quod"?'

'I mean just what I say. That someone who's been out of the way so long he thinks you can still get anywhere on a bus for tuppence hasn't been up in no North of England. He's been inside. I got ears in me head and unless you want me to tell her what I heard means, out you go.'

'Well,' Mrs Craggs said to Mrs Proost a few minutes later, taking care to stand where the old lady could see her lips. 'Well, I'm sure I don't know where he's gone. Upped and off he did, just like that. 'Spect he remembered an aeroplane he'd got to build or something.'

'Yes, yes. I expect that was it,' the old lady said. 'Young men like him have so much on their minds, you know.'

'Yes, dear – yes, madam,' said Mrs Craggs. 'That's true enough. And now shall I turn one of your musical boxes on for you? I expect you'd like to hear a nice cheerful tune.'

THE FIVE SENSES OF MRS CRAGGS
TOUCHING

ONE OF THE PLACES WHERE Mrs Craggs once worked was the Borough Museum in the town called Flinwich, and she was there at the time that the celebrated Golden Venus was on a week's loan exhibition. Indeed, she had the honour, obtained not without difficulty, of being allowed to dust this small but extremely ancient and valuable object.

At first, of course, no one had seen the necessity for carrying out such an everyday task. But when the Venus had been on its special display stand surrounded by its own rope barrier for some forty-eight hours, it became evident that even something as precious as this needed the attentions of the duster. Mr Slythe, the museum's assistant curator, had not been in favour of delegating this task to Mrs Craggs.

'But the Venus, but a charlady,' he had twittered. 'What if she did some damage? My mother's dailies are always breaking things. Always.'

Mrs Craggs stood there impassively, waiting to know whether or not she was going to be allowed to get on with it. And it was Mr Tovey, the curator himself, who gave the final go-ahead.

'Nonsense, man,' he said to Mr Slythe. 'The statue's solid metal, unharmed for over two thousand years, and you know how firmly it's fixed to the plinth. We both of us saw to that.'

'Ah, well, yes, I suppose so, I suppose so,' Mr Slythe agreed. And then he approached the statue for about the fiftieth time since it had been installed and started once more what Mrs Craggs called 'his cooing act'.

'Ah,' he said, 'the patina, the patina, the inimitable patina of age.'

If he'd said that once he'd said it twenty times, Mrs Craggs thought.

And then Mr Tovey, not to be outdone, approached the sacred work of art in his turn. And repeated what he had said some twenty times since it had been installed.

'The hand of genius, the unmistakable hand of genius Marvellous, magnificent, absolutely wonderful.'

'Shall I do it now, sir?' asked Mrs Craggs.

'Oh, very well, carry on then. Carry on.'

And both Mr Tovey and Mr Slythe turned away so as not to see Mrs Craggs's common yellow duster touch the product of the 'unmistakable hand of genius' or 'the patina of age'. And then they both slewed round again to make sure that, in spite of everything, Mrs Craggs was not wreaking havoc on the great work.

Indeed, the week of its exhibition was one of considerable strain for both the curator and his assistant. There was not only the public, which would keep coming and looking, attracted in numbers such as the museum had never seen before by stories in the papers about the immense value of the little golden statue, but there was the question of security at night. Of course, a firm of guards had been hired, and a pair of them made hourly patrols past the Golden Venus on its plinth while others were on duty at both the front and back doors. But Mr Tovey had decided this was not enough and had arranged with Mr Slythe that they should each spend half of every night of the exhibition week on the premises.

Both of them took every chance to point out to anybody who would listen, even to Mrs Craggs if no one better offered, what sacrifices of time they were making, and of saying simultaneously in their different ways that, of course, it was really no sacrifice at all to be able to spend hours in private contemplation either of 'the unmistakable hand of genius, coming down to us through the centuries' or of 'the patina, the wonderful patina of age, so fine yet so very, very enduring'.

So it could hardly be expected that neither of them would react with calm when, on the last morning of the Venus's stay in the museum, Mrs Craggs told them, one after the other, that the object over which she had just used her common yellow duster was not the genuine Golden Venus but a substitute.

She lay in wait first for Mr Tovey.

'I'm very sorry to have to tell you, sir,' she said when he re-entered the museum, 'that this is not the same statue as what I dusted yesterday.'

'What – what do you mean, woman? Not the same statue?'

'I can tell, sir. I can tell by the touch. I've dusted that five times in all since it's been here and I know the feel of it as well as I know the back of me own hand.'

'We'll have a look at this,' Mr Tovey declared.

And he took the steps two a time up to the landing where the Golden Venus stood. He drew a long breath and glared hard at the statue, then rounded on Mrs Craggs.

'Piffle, my good woman,' he said. 'Sheer and utter piffle. Why, you've only to look to see the hand of genius there, the unmistakable hand of genius.'

'And you've only got to lay a duster on it to know it's not the same as what it was yesterday,' Mrs Craggs declared, with equal firmness.

Mr Tovey drew himself up. But he did not pour forth the torrent of words Mrs Craggs had braced herself for. Instead he suddenly thrust his big round face close to hers and spoke in a low whisper.

'Now, listen to me, my good woman, you are wrong. You cannot be anything else. I have a lifetime of knowledge behind me when I tell you that statue *is* the Golden Venus. But I know what the Press is and what reporters are capable of. So, understand this, you are not to breathe one word of even the possibility of a theft. Not one word.'

Mrs Craggs looked doubtful. But Mr Tovey was a persuasive man and at last she mumbled agreement. Yet, thinking the matter over, she came to the conclusion that his prohibition ought not to include his fellow art expert, Mr Slythe. So she waited her chance and at last managed to corner the assistant curator at a spot not far from the Golden Venus, during a slack period in the museum's unaccustomedly busy life.

'Can I have a word?' she asked.

'Yes, yes. What is it? What is it now? Always something. Always some pettifogging detail preventing one from concentrating on one's true work.'

'Well, if you say that someone putting a dummy in place of that Golden Venus is a detail,' Mrs Craggs answered, 'then that's your privilege. But I think it ought to be gone into.'

Mr Slythe was even more upset than Mr Tovey. He scooted over the stone floor toward the statue as if he had been unexpectedly put on roller skates and he peered at it with such fearful intensity that he might almost have melted it. And then he returned, white-faced, to Mrs Craggs. But not with dismay. With anger.

'You wretched, wretched person,' he said. 'How dare you? How dare you say a thing like that to me? It's enough to give me a nervous breakdown. Yes, a nervous breakdown.'

'Then you don't think it has been changed?' Mrs Craggs said.

'I do not. Why, anyone with a grain of sensibility could see that *pièce* has the patina of age on every inch of it. The unmistakable patina of age. And you tell me that it is a substitute.'

And Mr Slythe wheeled round and marched away to the sanctuary of his private office.

Mrs Craggs ought to have been convinced. But, if she was, then why was it that she came to the museum the evening after the immensely successful Golden Venus exhibition had been triumphantly concluded and put in a good many hours of overtime, unpaid? She got out her dustcloths and worked away, rubbing and polishing stairs and corridors, showcases and display rooms. The museum had never gleamed so in all its days.

And at last her prowling duster encountered what she had thought that it would. In next to no time she was out on the steps of the building looking up and down the street, and before long she saw what she was looking for – the local police constable passing on his beat. She beckoned to him.

'I want to report a theft,' she said.

The constable hurried in and Mrs Craggs led him to the place where, dusting and polishing, she had come across a loose tile in the wall decoration of one of the rooms.

'Look,' she said.

And she prised out the tile and the one next to it, to reveal a long cavity in which, reposing on a layer of cottonwool, was nothing less than the real Golden Venus.

'It was changed over during one of the gaps between the security patrols,' Mrs Craggs declared.

The constable, who had been aware of the precautions taken over so valuable a piece of property on his beat, saw at once what the situation was.

'It must have been one of them two,' he said. 'The whatsit-curator, Mr Tovey, or his Number Two, Mr Slythe. One of them must have hidden it here till he could slip it out. But – but which? They were each on guard alone half the night. Which could it be?'

'That's simple enough,' Mrs Craggs replied. 'They both of them told me I was an old fool for saying it had been changed over. But only one of them made a fuss about not telling anyone else. It's the "unmistakable hand of genius" you've got to go for, not "the patina of age".'

THE FIVE SENSES OF MRS CRAGGS
TASTING

One of the things Mrs Craggs had to do when, in what you might call her Flinwich days, she was Mrs Fitzblaney's daily help, was to stay late every Thursday evening and take up supper to Mrs Fitzblaney's husband, the old Colonel, who was bedridden. 'Thirty years between them two if there's a day,' Mrs Craggs used to say to Mrs Milhorne. But she got well paid for this extra work, time and half always. She had been quite firm about that the moment she was first asked, since she well knew there was money and to spare in that household. The Colonel always had the best and liked the best, there was no doubt about that. Though there was doubt about the Colonel himself. The doctor had said years before that he might go any day, and every time that Mrs Craggs came to the house she half expected to hear the worst.

But every Thursday evening Mrs Fitzblaney went off to her art class. 'And holding hands with the art master, if all I hear's true,' said Mrs Craggs. 'Still, that's no business of mine. A little of what you fancy don't do you no harm, that's my motto.'

And every week Mrs Fitzblaney left behind her two ounces of Patna rice, to be boiled for ten minutes by the clock and no more, and a saucepan of ready-prepared curry to be heated up.

'Fair fussy he is about his curry, the old boy,' Mrs Craggs would say. It had to be cooked in the afternoon by Mrs Fitzblaney in exactly the right way, and all Mrs Craggs had to do was to see that she knocked on the bedroom door, with the tray in her hands, at eight o'clock to the second.

She had been late once, but only once. At half a minute past eight the Colonel's voice, despite his illness, had come roaring down the stairs. 'Bearer! Bearer! Where's that blasted bearer? Fellow's late on parade. I won't have it.' Very much on her dignity Mrs Craggs had been when she went in with the tray that night.

But being on the dot was not all. That curry had to be hot as well. Not spicy hot. The Colonel liked it good and fiery, but there the doctor had put his foot down. But as near boiling hot as dammit that curry had to be. There had been trouble about that once too.

'Bearer, what the hell's this? Bloody *ice* pudding? Eh, man? Eh?'

'I do my best,' Mrs Craggs had replied. 'And what's more, if I may make so bold as to mention, I am not a man, nor yet a bearer neither, whatever that may be.'

But all the same ever afterwards she took the precaution of dipping a finger into the saucepan and having a taste, when she thought the curry was ready, to make sure it had reached a really hot heat. The stuff was nasty enough, she thought, but she was not going to be called names at her age.

And then one Thursday came and, as Mrs Craggs said later to Mrs Milhorne, 'I will not forget that day, not so long as I has breath in my body to remember by.'

At the start it did not seem to be different from any other Thursday evening. Mrs Craggs, who came to the house to do the cleaning in the afternoon, got through her work as usual. It was the sitting room on Thursdays, and the hall. And at just the usual time Mrs Fitzblaney came down the stairs dressed as usual in her painting things – 'Pair of jeans that should've been in the dustbin years ago,' said Mrs Craggs. 'And too tight for her by a long chalk where I won't mention' – and as usual Mrs

Fitzblaney fussed over telling Mrs Craggs what she knew perfectly well already.

'You won't forget to be on the dot of eight with his supper, will you, Mrs Er –?' – 'Never did have the common decency to get me name right, but that was Mrs Fitzblaney all over,' said Mrs Craggs – and no sooner had Mrs Craggs assured her that she had no need to worry about that than it was 'Oh, and Mrs Er –, I forgot to say. You will make quite sure the curry's hot, won't you? The Colonel gets so cross if it isn't just to his liking, you know, and it's terribly bad for him to – to – Well, you know, lose his temper.'

'There won't be no cause for complaint from me,' said Mrs Craggs.

And there was not. At 7.40 to the second – she had the radio on 'dead quiet' to make sure – on to the stove went the water for the rice and on too went the curry over a nice low heat. And at 7.55 precisely Mrs Craggs had the rice dished and waiting and was making doubly sure the curry was really hot. She put her finger in, winced at the heat, but nevertheless lifted a yellowy-brown gob to her lips and bravely tasted it.

'Hot as hot,' she said to herself. 'Old Blood-and-Guts'll have no complaints tonight.' Then she poured the curry with care on to the centre of the hollowed-out mound of rice, put the plate on the tray, and carried it upstairs. The Colonel never ate a dessert. 'Blasted sweet stuff. Nobody wants to put that in their mouth,' he used to say.

Mrs Craggs knocked at the door of the bedroom just as she heard the church clock strike eight, and 'Come in, come in,' the Colonel shouted. Mrs Craggs entered, carried the food over to the bed-tray which was already on parade over the Colonel's knees, and set it down.

'Hm,' grunted the Colonel. And then he had the grace to add, 'Hah. Thank you.' Mrs Craggs knew her services were not required any longer and down she went to the kitchen.

She ought really at this point to have put on her hat and coat and left. The Colonel always pushed aside his tray when he had finished and Mrs Fitzblaney brought it downstairs when she got back from the art class. That was the regular routine. The Colonel objected to 'blasted women always coming in and out of the room like a set of damn railway trains'.

But tonight something stopped Mrs Craggs as she went to take her hat off the peg on the back of the kitchen door. It was not anything particular, just a feeling – a feeling that something was not quite as it ought to be.

For perhaps a full half-minute she stood there, nose up against her coat as it hung on the peg, the hat held high in her hand. And then she got it.

'Hot,' she said. 'It was too hot. Spicy hot as can be.' And then she dropped her hat on the floor just where she stood, wheeled round and was out of the kitchen and thumping off up the stairs in as little time as it takes to tell. She got to the top of the stairs. She made for the Colonel's door. She thrust it open without so much as a knock or a word of apology and said, 'Stop!'

'Stop? Stop? What the hell d'you mean by "stop"?'

* * *

Afterwards Mrs Craggs said to Mrs Milhorne that she had never seen a man look so astonished. 'You'd have thought it was the Angel Gabriel come in,' she said. 'You would have, honest.'

But at the time Mrs Craggs failed to answer the Colonel's question. Instead she fired one of her own. 'That curry,' she said, 'have you tasted any of it?'

'Of course I've tasted my bloody curry, woman,' the Colonel thundered back. 'What's the infernal stuff for if it isn't to be tasted?'

'Then don't you eat one bit more,' said Mrs Craggs.

'What blasted nonsense is this? The first decent hot curry I've had in the last five years and you have the abominable impertinence to come in here and tell me to stop eating it. I'll do no such thing.'

And the Colonel plunged his fork deep into the

browny-yellow concoction and lifted a gigantic quantity, all dripping, toward his mouth.

It was then that Mrs Craggs did an unforgivable thing. She launched herself across the room toward the bed and knocked the Colonel's full fork flying.

'What the —'

Words failed the colonel.

'Oh, sir,' said Mrs Craggs, 'I'm sorry. I really am. I don't know how I even dared to do it, sir.'

'And nor do I, you infernal harridan. You're dismissed, d'you hear? Get out, do y'hear me, get out!'

But it was at that moment that the Colonel began to be seriously ill. Mrs Craggs rolled up her sleeves and set to, and the doctor said afterwards that it was solely owing to the sensible way she went about it that the Colonel came out of it as well as he did. But, as she said to Mrs Milhorne, 'I wasn't exactly as calm as a tuppenny cucumber at the time.'

In fact, she had gabbled and babbled and said a lot of things that hardly made sense, all of which had had the effect of calming down the old Colonel and probably saving him to live out the rest of his life as the happy resident of a nursing home for ex-officers with proper batmen in attendance.

'It was it being so hot, sir,' Mrs Crags had babbled that evening. 'I mean I know it has to be hot. But not hot like that. And I know Mrs Fitzblaney knows it mustn't be, 'cos she's always telling me so. And then, when I realised that it was too hot, spicy hot I mean, all of a sudden it come over me why it was. And only why. Poison, I thought. It's to hide the taste of poison. She's done it. She's aiming to be off with that artist fellow and live in comfort on what she got in the will. Well, a little of what you fancy does you good, but there's some things goes too far. And murder's one.'

Yes, yes. Very interesting. But, of course, Mrs Craggs worked in more glamorous places than — er — Flinwich. I mean, didn't she once work in Fleet Street?

We both of us assisted in The Street, as I like to call it. Only I was with what you might call one of the better-known papers. Mrs Craggs was elsewhere.

Yes. So I believe. Now, if we could get the editor when she was there to come on the show … Did she ever bump into him, do you know?

Bump into. She did more than that, if what I got to hear's true. You know, Mrs Craggs has got a wicked sense of humour sometimes. Real wicked.

IV

Mrs Craggs and the Living Dead

ONCE SOME TIME AGO, Mrs Craggs had a job with the greatest newspaper in the world. She was not its Fashion Editor – indeed, in those days it turned up its mighty nose at the notion of anything as frivolous as fashion, let alone a Fashion Editor – but she felt her job was one which had to be done and which contributed its share to the proper conduct of the austere sheet which appeared every morning to be lapped up in clubs and Cabinet offices and places where grave opinions gravely stated count. Mrs Craggs, of course, never read this sheet. She preferred something with pictures. 'Well,' she would say, 'I like a bit o' sauce, an' I don't care who knows it.' Her job on the greatest newspaper in the world was to clean and polish the first-floor offices during the mornings when hardly anybody was there. She worked under the general supervision of Mrs Gollond, the Chief Domestic Assistant. But she herself had no title, resounding or otherwise. And, she sometimes thought, she washed floors and polished them rather better than Mrs Gollond, for all that lady's distinguished office.

One of the things that Mrs Craggs liked best about this job was that nothing ever happened. Mrs Milhorne had a job at the same time on the newspaper which she and Mrs Craggs preferred, and things were different there, if only half what Mrs

Milhorne confided to her in the Tube on the way home was true. There, there were sudden sackings and meteoric promotions – 'Why,' said Mrs Milhorne, 'them little name-boards outside their offices, they go up and down so fast it seems like they take them out o' your very 'ands while you're giving them a bit of a dust' – and there were blazing rows, and there were reporters coming in at the last second with scoops, and murderers wanting to confess, and photographs that no one would dare to print, except that they did. But at the greatest newspaper in the world all was always calm. And they had very nice plain green lino which took polish just a treat.

So it was really quite something to cause a flutter when one morning, as Mrs Craggs and Mrs Gollond were giving the third office on the left as you went down the main corridor a thorough turn-out – 'It's a wonder where all the dust comes from,' said Mrs Craggs. 'We always has dust 'ere,' retorted Mrs Gollond, 'always have and always will' – who should come almost rushing in, insofar as anyone ever rushed in those high-ceilinged offices and corridors, but the Editor himself.

He certainly entered the room abruptly. And then he looked about him as if the presence of the two ladies was altogether unexpected.

But in a moment he recovered himself.

'Ah,' he said. 'Ah. Ah, good morning, Mrs Gollond.'

He knew Mrs Gollond by name. Everyone knew Mrs Gollond by name. She had worked at the paper for longer than almost anybody else. And she made sure that they never forgot.

'Good morning,' she said to the Editor, putting into the words the plain hint that it was now less of a good morning for his having come in and disturbed the rhythm of her task.

'Yes,' said the Editor. 'Yes. Well, you see … You see, I was looking for Mr Parmenter. I heard at a dinner last night that the Duke of Holderness is not at all well and I thought that – er – we should be making sure of the obit, you know.'

'I dare say,' said Mrs Gollond.

And she sniffed.

'But that don't alter the fac',' she said, 'that it's not yet gorn half-past ten and it's well known, by me if it ain't by nobody else, that Mr Parmenter don't never come in afore twelve.'

'Oh, yes,' said the Editor. 'Yes, quite. But ... But I was wondering about young Hipworthy – it is Mr Hipworthy, isn't it? – is he by any chance anywhere about?'

'As for Mr Hipworthy,' Mrs Gollond pronounced, 'I can't be saying, neither one way nor the other. Mr Hipworthy ain't what you might call regular. Not the way we likes 'em regular here.'

'Well, no. No, I suppose not. A little young, perhaps. Yes, yes. Well, if you do see him, ask him to step round to my office, would you? And good day, Mrs Gollond.'

The Editor smiled, as if it cost him an effort. And then he cast a look in Mrs Craggs's direction.

'Er – good day,' he said.

'Good day, sir,' said Mrs Craggs. 'And we'll be sure to tell him. Don't you worry.'

'Tell him we will or tell him we won't,' said Mrs Gollond as soon as the door was shut, and perhaps just a fraction before. 'Coming in here at this time. I don't know what he thinks he's thinking of.'

'Well, it was something to do with the Duke of Holderness,' Mrs Craggs said, seeming to be a little less quick on the uptake than she usually was. 'The Duke of Holderness and his obit. Whatever an obit is.'

'An obit,' said Mrs Gollond, speaking with all the authority that her long, long service had imbued her with, 'an obit is what you might call a report an' account of the living dead.'

'Oh, yes?' said Mrs Craggs. 'And what might that be when it's at 'ome?'

Mrs Gollond looked at her, as if it was just possible that she was being disrespectful.

'It's what we writes about 'em when they're gorn,' she explained, as soon as the impossible notion had been swept from her mind. 'We kind o' sums 'em up like. Tells 'em what they did wrong, an' if they did right. An' it's the length what counts, it's the length what counts in the end. Do they weigh up

73

to the full column? Or do they come under it? There's many a
man walking the corridors o' Parliament this minute what
would wish an' wish with all his might he was going to come up
to the full column. But he ain't.'

Mrs Craggs listened to the doom pronounced in her usual
impassive manner.

'Ah, well,' she said after a short pause. 'This ain't a-getting Mr
Parmenter's desk dusted, nor yet young Mr Hipworthy's table.'

And she turned, whether by way of expressing a preference
which might run dead counter to Mrs Gollond's scale of values
or not it was hard to tell, to deal first with the solid but humble
corner table allotted to young Mr Hipworthy.

Mrs Gollond advanced on Mr Parmenter's desk, plainly
feeling that a due order of precedence was being maintained.
But, hardly had she got to work bundling up the papers on the
desk's surface into piles of a neatness and shape which she
considered proper, than she stopped with a horrified intake of
breath.

'He's done it again,' she announced.

'What? Old Parmenter?'

'Old Mr Parmenter, if you please. Mr Parmenter of the
Obituary Department. Leave his keys a-dangling just anywhere
he may, but he's Mr Parmenter still. Just so long as he's in this
office. And that won't end all in a minute. Not 'ere, it won't.'

'Why,' said Mrs Craggs, 'won't he go and get the sack then, for
carelessness, leaving his keys the way he does?'

And she innocently polished away at the edge of young Mr
Hipworthy's heavy old table.

'The sack?' said Mrs Gollond. 'The sack? Here? You don't
know what you're talking about, my good woman. The sack?
From this place? Listen, nobody ain't never been dismissed even
from here. Much less get the sack. Oh dear, oh dear, you ain't
got no idea, you ain't. Not no idea.'

Mrs Craggs went on polishing for a little, working her way
now round the clutter of odds and ends and scraps of this and
scraps of that littering the table. But after a while she asked
another question.

'Not even young Mr Hipworthy?' she said. 'Wouldn't he even ever get dismissed? The way he goes on? Coming in at all hours? And playing jokes on people who've been here long before he so much as saw the light o' day.'

There had been an occasion when young Mr Hipworthy had glued down a duster which Mrs Gollond had chanced to leave on his table, and the repercussions of that had not easily been forgotten.

Mrs Gollond sighed.

'No,' she said, 'not even young Mr Hipworthy, though if I had my way he'd be the first it'd happen to. The first.'

And there was no doubt that Mrs Gollond thought that she ought to have her way on the greatest newspaper in the world.

* * *

It was perhaps a good thing it had been that day on which Mrs Craggs had received instruction on the exact meaning and moral worth of an obit. Because, just as she was coming out of the back entrance on her way to Blackfriars Underground station, a gentleman came up to her and broached that very topic.

'Good day, madam.'

'Good day,' said Mrs Craggs.

She could have said 'Good day, Mr Sundukian' because she had recognised in an instant the portly, spade-bearded, flashing-monocled figure of the notorious, high-living, high-spending financier, Kevork Sundukian. Mr Sundukian's photograph appeared in the newspaper Mrs Craggs favoured almost as frequently as the photographs that bannered the 'bit o' sauce' she liked. Occasionally, indeed, the two were conjoined, though Mr Sundukian's bits of sauce always had a whiff of the cultural about them since he was a prodigal outpourer of funds for unusual operatic ventures and for musical events centring on ladies with wonderful voices and dazzling physiques.

But Mrs Craggs just said 'Good day' and waited to see what would happen.

'You work for that splendid journal, I perceive,' said Mr Sundukian, casting a glance at the mellow brick pile behind them.

'Yes,' said Mrs Craggs.

'I envy you, madam. I envy you. I will not disguise from you that I am a wealthy man' – You'd better not, thought Mrs Craggs – 'but I tell you frankly I wish it had been my lot to find an occupation inside those walls. Even of the most simple. Even perhaps the chap who polishes the linoleum there.'

'Well, that ain't a chap,' Mrs Craggs said.

'No, madam?'

'That's me. Or, it is for all the first floor of the place.'

'Ah, I envy you. The first floor. Where I believe the Editor himself has his office. Do you – tell me, madam, does it fall to you actually to polish the linoleum in that august sanctuary?'

'I don't know about August,' said Mrs Craggs, 'I has my two weeks 'oliday August. But I polishes that floor, yes. And messed up terrible with cigarette burns it is behind the desk there. Terrible.'

'That's sad, madam. Bad even. But, tell me, do you also by any chance have to – er – deal with the office where they file the – ahem – obituary notices?'

'I do,' said Mrs Craggs, who seldom saw any harm in the truth.

'Ah, what a place that must be. What a place. Those accounts of men's lives. Those accounts they will never see, but which the whole world will read the day after their deaths. Remarkable.'

'Could do with a new table in the corner,' said Mrs Craggs. 'Why, the one they got's so old you can't get the dust out of its nooks and crannies, not no how.'

'Indeed? Remarkable. And the filing cabinets, are they equally ancient too? Deficient locks, that sort of thing?'

'No. They locks up all right. It's the chap what keeps the keys that's on the ancient side there. Leaves 'em anywhere, he do. Anywhere.'

'Indeed? Indeed? So I suppose it would not really be

difficult for anyone with access to that room at a quiet hour to read a particular "obit" – is that what they call them in the jargon? An obit? To quietly peruse one of those? Even to – ahem – abstract it?'

'I s'pose you mean pinch it?' said Mrs Craggs.

Mr Sundukian smiled through his great spade of a beard. It was a sudden explosion of charm that had on one particular occasion netted him no less a sum than three-quarters of a million pounds on one single delicate deal.

'Why, yes, madam,' he said. 'You hit it exactly. Would it be easy enough, if there were a willing agent, to "pinch" a particular obit?'

''Course it would,' said Mrs Craggs.

Mr Sundukian's spade beard opened in another smile.

'Then let me be frank, madam,' he said. 'The obit in question is that of Mr Kevork Sundukian. The agent in question, I devoutly hope, is yourself. And there could be any reasonable sum of money in question, as a consideration. Twenty pounds, shall we say?'

'Take money to do that?' said Mrs Craggs. 'I got more pride.'

Mr Sundukian stopped in his tracks and laid a hand, dashingly manicured, on Mrs Craggs's coat sleeve, threadbare but still ready to keep out a winter's cold.

'Madam,' he said, 'forgive a crass old man. I knew at the very moment I saw you that an approach that mentioned money was out of the question. But I am a financier, madam. I think money. I live money. I cannot help but approach any question in terms of money. Yet I should have known there are people in the world who are better than I am. I should have known that.'

Mrs Craggs blew down her nose, a little like a horse.

'Madam,' said Mr Sundukian, letting go her coat sleeve. 'Allow me to tell you about myself. Let me for once unlock those steel-barred doors that a financier learns to guard himself with from his earliest days. Madam, I am a vain man.'

'Well, o' course you are,' Mrs Craggs agreed.

The spade beard closed then like a great trap. But almost at once it opened again to reveal a smile that was tenderly beguiling, waif-like almost.

'Yes, vain,' sighed Mr Sundukian. 'Vain and anxious. Anxious about what the world thinks of a man who, though he has done his share to make the world a richer place, and more than his share perhaps, is still concerned that he may be thought of, be labelled even, as no more than a machine for making money.'

He paused. He looked at Mrs Craggs.

'Madam,' he said, 'do you see my position?'

'Yes,' said Mrs Craggs, because she did.

'Then, madam, can I dare to hope? I have trodden on your finer feelings with a truly brutal heel. I know it. I regret it. Bitterly. But, madam, can I appeal to those feelings now? Madam, I desire with all the force that is in me to know what that great newspaper will tell the world about me on the day after my death. Madam, will you … May I beg you to indulge an old, vain and suffering man?'

'Well,' said Mrs Craggs, looking at the eyes above that spade of a beard which was cut now by the ribbon of a fallen monocle. 'Well, if I could, I would. I tells you that. But I can't. You knows I can't, don't you? And if I can't, I can't.'

A swift and forcefully manicured hand brought the monocle flashing up to the right eye again.

'A thousand pounds?' said Mr Sundukian.

He got no answer. The monocle twinkled sharply.

'Two thousand?'

The monocle glittered with ferocity.

'Five thousand? Five thousand pounds for that strip of paper?'

The monocle glared.

'Madam, you're a fool. A damned, ignorant, stupid fool.'

And Mr Sundukian jumped into a huge, sliding, gleaming limousine that, at a click of a dashingly manicured hand, had materialised beside him. Mrs Craggs turned towards the Underground.

She decided not to talk to Mrs Milhorne about what had happened. She did not altogether trust Mrs Milhorne's tender susceptibilities.

* * *

That might have been that, had it not been for Mrs Craggs's fradgetting over the engrained dust in the nooks and crannies of the old table in the corner of the Obituary Department which was all that young Mr Hipworthy had to call his own. There was one particularly packed seam at the top of the thick right-hand leg that had seemed one day as if it was at last going to yield up its riches. It had not quite. But, as Mrs Craggs had been twisting her polishing mop into the cigarette-pocked lino behind the Editor's desk it had suddenly occurred to her that the corner of a duster well moistened with spit might after all do the trick. So she went back to the Obituary office.

And caught Mrs Gollond in the act.

Mrs Gollond had in her hand Mr Parmenter's bunch of keys, which no doubt he had left dangling once again in one of the drawers of his desk, and she had open the big old mahogany-fronted filing drawer on which, in a brass holder, there was a yellowed card bearing the solitary letter 'S'. She had even had one of the long obituary proofs half-way out of its place when Mrs Craggs had opened the door. If Mrs Craggs had stopped to wet the corner of her duster before she had gone in, as she had considered doing, the five-thousand-pound strip of paper might have been in the pocket of Mrs Gollond's flowered apron.

But, as it was, Mrs Gollond simply stuffed it in haste back into its place, slammed the drawer shut and began furiously rubbing at its mahogany surface with her duster.

'I see Mr Parmenter's left his keys again,' said Mrs Craggs.

Mrs Gollond drew herself up.

'He has,' she declared. 'And it's not good enough. There's house rules and there's house rules, and them's what's got to be obeyed. I shall speak to the Editor.'

And that was when Mrs Craggs decided that really and truly it was not good enough. Mrs Gollond had gone too far. It was time something was done.

So, as soon as young Mr Hipworthy came in, she had a quiet word with him.

'I think it's a jolly good wheeze,' said young Mr Hipworthy.

* * *

The calm days went by in the office of the greatest newspaper in the world. The Duke of Holderness died and his updated obituary came to one column and a third, *Services to Agriculture and Philately*. Daily in the Tube on the way home Mrs Milhorne gave Mrs Craggs gory details, of instant sackings, of one Editor for half an afternoon, and of what the Crime Reporter had found on his desk – 'I come over so queer I 'ad to go next door for a rum an' peppermint' – after an individual in a shabby macintosh had been allowed incautiously to wait for twenty minutes in his room. But Mrs Craggs had nothing to offer in return.

Till, one day about three weeks later, there was an event that broke the great newspaper's calm in no uncertain manner. Mr Kevork Sundukian entered by the front door flourishing, even brandishing, an enormous whip and demanding to see the Editor.

But of course you cannot horsewhip the Editor of the greatest newspaper in the world any more than you could have cocked a snook at the Prophet Moses. So, after a short interval, all that happened was that a conversation took place between the irate financier and the Editor, the latter flanked as a precautionary measure by the Court Correspondent, who was a former Welsh International Rugby forward, and one of the sub-editors from the Sports Department, hastily summoned and carrying with a certain casualness a cricket bat autographed by the Oxford University team who in 1877 had scored a total of only twelve runs against the MCC, an item that had reposed in a corner of the Sports sub-editors' room for full many a year. He was a somewhat weedy fellow, but a staunch believer in *Wisden's Cricketer's Almanac* and a bit of gossip as well.

It was through him, indeed, that it became known all round the building that the Editor had told Mr Sundukian in round terms that, whether the rather short obituary notice which he had brought to his attention – *Mr Kevork Sundukian. A Money-Making Machine* – was or was not a true copy of what would appear in the paper on the day after Mr Sundukian's decease, 'and, of course, we all – er – hope that will not be for many a long year yet', it had beyond doubt been obtained by Mr Sundukian in a fraudulent manner and that was absolutely unacceptable.

When Mr Sundukian, on his way out, had been offered back his whip by the young lady from the Advertisement Department's counter into whose safekeeping it had been put, he had donated it, it was reported, to that young lady, but not in a very gracious manner.

Thereafter certain discreet inquiries had been made, by none other than the Manager of the great newspaper himself. In the course of them young Mr Hipworthy had mentioned that he had one evening sketched out a small piece of writing in the form of an obituary and that a friend in the Composing Room had, as it happened, set it up in type. But, he had assured the Manager, now once more in its allotted space in the file marked 'S' there reposed the paper's considered comment, measuring nearly but not quite one full column, on *Mr Kevork Sundukian. Patronage of the Musical Arts.* At the end of the Manager's inquiries Mrs Gollond was peremptorily dismissed, even though dismissals were not very frequent occurrences in the office.

Well, Mrs Craggs had thought when she heard the news, this will be something to tell Mrs Milhorne.

But she did not tell her friend about a short conversation that took place next day. The Editor, coming early into his office, found her twisting and twisting her polishing mop into the cigarette burns on the floor behind his desk.

'Ah – er – yes, Mrs Craggs,' he said. 'Yes. Well, she always was a beastly woman, wasn't she? I'm – er – awfully glad you did what you – er – did.'

Mrs Milhorne. Mrs Milhorne.

And, as I was saying, I —

Mrs Milhorne.

Yaiss? Was there somethink you wanted to know? I'm sure I can oblige. There's no one knows more —

Well, can you tell me if there's a Mr Craggs? I mean, what does he do? Or is he dead, actually?

Well. Well, I'm never quite sure whether he's still around or whether he's gorn, Alf. You don't hear much about him. But you don't ever hear he's definitely passed on. I just wish somebody'd make up their mind, that's all. I mean, I know my Milhorne's still with us, though I must say I don't know from one time to another whether he's orf somewhere and I have to be prostrated on me chaise longoo or whether he's sort of 'overing in the background. Hovering, I should say. Pardon me, hovering.

Yes. But if Mrs Craggs tells you as much as you say she does, surely —

I mean, Milhorne was definitely away that time Mrs Craggs got that job You-know-where. And I was definitely on my chaise longoo then. Otherwise I might of ... Well, I might of 'appened, happened, to talk to You-know-who.

V

MRS CRAGGS AND A CERTAIN LADY'S TOWN HOUSE

WITH ONE LADY IN LONDON for whom Mrs Craggs worked briefly she had to sign a piece of paper, very thick and creamy and printed in big black lettering, before she could start the job at all. In it she promised she would never divulge any information she might learn in the course of her employment under pain of various fearsome penalties.

Mrs Craggs had hesitated about signing because one of the reasons she was thinking of taking the job was so as she could pass on some inside details to Mrs Milhorne, who at that time was in such a state of distress (owing to the sudden departure, once again, of Mr Milhorne) that she felt herself unable so much as to put duster to furniture for anybody – 'What'd do her most good,' said Mrs Craggs, 'is polish a nice big stretch o' lino, nothing like bringing up a good shine on lino to get you over the 'ump' – but she reckoned in any case that just to tell her friend that she had noticed the lady out in the morning walking her corgi dogs or something like that could do nobody any harm. And she was not even going to get into the place itself, just into the gardens.

The job which there was all the fuss about was only a temporary one, providing extra help on certain days when there were garden parties. The parties the lady gave were easily the biggest in London, 'and posh,' said Mrs Craggs afterwards.

'They were so posh there, how any of 'em could ever have swallowed down a good hot cuppa an' a nice piece o' chocolate cake is more nor I could say.'

So, although she hesitated, in the end Mrs Craggs signed the paper, and with a good conscience. But before the job was done, and it lasted only one day – she never went back – she had learned a dreadful secret indeed, one which she was to take very good care that Mrs Milhorne never got even the slightest hint of. It would have had her up off the old couch in her front room – 'the chaise longoo', Mrs Milhorne never failed to call it – and away to Fleet Street before you could say 'miracle cure'.

Mrs Craggs had not been in the gardens there half an hour when she got her first inkling that everything in those gardens was not as lovely as it should be, despite many assurances from Mrs Milhorne. She had been busy sweeping the wooden floor of the first of the huge marquees to be erected, and incidentally had already collected enough gossip from her fellow workers to keep Mrs Milhorne happy on her chaise longoo for a twelvemonth, if she felt on consideration it was proper to pass it on.

All them corgis 'aving to be rounded up first thing and kep' out o' the way in case they bites a guest, she thought, now is that something I could be sent to prison for, or ain't it?

Then a single small snag occurred in the smooth running of the preparations. A signboard proclaiming 'Tea Tent' which had just been taken from the box in which it had rested ever since the final garden party of the year before was found to be smeared with a great smudge of sticky black mud. Where that had come from no one could say. But, more urgently, at this stage of the proceedings there was no handy supply of water with which to wash it off.

'See to it, would you, Mrs – Er,' said the tenting manager, and away he went before any awkward questions could be asked.

Mrs Craggs knew that to go indoors and hunt about until she found a sink, though it would no doubt be easy enough, was simply not to be done. So she took a good look all round her and in a minute spotted, through a clump of trees, the gleam of water.

Be a pond or a stream or a lake even, she thought to herself. And, securely gripping the elegantly painted sign, off she went.

Sure enough, just beyond a big clump of a plant (which Mrs Craggs recognised with a start of pleasure in these exalted surroundings as being a homely growth known to her mother before her as Devil's Snitchbane and very handy for putting a branch or two of in places where it ponged a bit), there was a lake. It was long and narrow with a pretty-looking low bridge across it, just like in the country, and three or four long-legged pink flamingoes pecking about, beautiful as a picture. Mrs Craggs gave a sigh of relief. It seemed her difficult task would soon be neatly completed. Until she saw the soldier.

And what a soldier he was. No ordinary bloke in a khaki uniform whom Mrs Craggs might have felt she could go up to and confide her problem in, but a magnificent creature – more like a painted statue, Mrs Craggs thought, nor a chap as'd want to 'ave a good scratch every now an' again – dressed in a faultless scarlet jacket, immaculately creased and immensely long black trousers, with a belt pipeclayed to a whiteness more dazzling than snow and brass buttons shining more brightly than the sun overhead, and above all crowned by a towering softly gleaming beautiful black bearskin. He was standing just on the far side of the little bridge, sternly regarding alternately the elegant, long-necked, pink-breasted flamingoes near him and the distant high brick wall which surrounded the whole gardens. On guard. On duty. Important. Not to be spoken to. Or even smiled at. Much, much less asked if it was all right to wash a signboard in the lake over which, ramrod stiff, he was presiding.

Mrs Craggs stood, just in the shadow of the big clump of Devil's Snitchbane, and looked at him and wondered what she was going to do now.

And then two quite unexpected things happened. First, the statue soldier suddenly seemed to slump to only about three-quarters of his previously imposing height and take a quick – and, yes, furtive – glance all round about him before in one swift movement he plucked off his magnificent bearskin, laid it on the ground just behind him, pulled out a handkerchief from under his scarlet jacket and gave a good mop to the sweat which must have collected on his scalp and forehead under the heat of the already brilliant sun. And, second, from out of a dense bush of purple-spiked buddleia nearby at just that moment there emerged, almost as startling as the sight of the guardsman's sudden alteration, what was plainly nothing other than a corgi dog.

And, worse, hardly had Mrs Craggs had time to reflect that almost certainly it would be a betrayal of that solemn piece of thick and creamy paper to tell Mrs Milhorne that even the loftiest canine arrangements sometimes went astray, when the little dog took one good sniff at the bearskin lying on the ground just in front of him and lifted his leg.

Mrs Craggs rushed forward from the shadow of the clump of Snitchbane.

'Hey! Stop! Stop that, you little brute,' she yelled.

The little brute may have been accustomed to receiving orders from very much higher up in the social scale, but perhaps he had not before had any given him quite so vigorously. Because he took one quick look at Mrs Craggs, coming tearing over a verdant sward towards him, and he vanished.

Mrs Craggs went up to the soldier.

'Well, 'ere's a how-d'ye-do,' she said. 'Messed your titfer up right proper, he has, the little bleeder.'

'What am I going to do?'

The soldier, for all his scarlet jacket, bright-shining brass and dazzling pipeclayed belt, was no longer a figure of untouchable statue-prestige. He was something Mrs Craggs recognised very well: a small boy in a stew.

'Well, we could dip it in the water,' she suggested cheerfully, giving the polluted bearskin an appraising look.

'And ruin it?' gasped the soldier. 'I'd be in the glasshouse as long as I lived.'

'We could try giving it a bit of a brush wi' some grass or something.'

'But it'd smell,' the guardsman objected. 'I'm not going to be stuck out here all day keeping an eye on a lot of blooming flamingoes. I got to go and direct guests out the front first thing this afternoon.'

'Yeh,' said Mrs Craggs, unable to keep back a bit of a grin, 'you'd direct 'em just about the wrong way, whiffing like that.'

'It ain't no laughing matter,' the soldier retorted, a look of real agony on his martial visage. 'I'm done for. I'm up the creek. I'm down the pan.'

'Oh, no, you ain't,' Mrs Craggs said, half sharply, half cheeringly.

'But I must be. On parade and ponging like the back-end of nowhere.'

'But you won't pong,' said Mrs Craggs. 'Not with a nice leaf or two of Devil's Snitchbane under your 'at, you won't.'

'Devil's Snitchbane? What the devil's that?'

So Mrs Craggs explained. And the plant – what reverberating Latin name it bore to the lady's many gardeners heaven only knew – was duly ransacked for a good bunch of its subtly aromatic leaves and these were quickly stuffed into the guardsman's tall and desecrated bearskin, and before another five minutes had passed Mrs Craggs, sniffing the air round about like a vacuum-cleaner, pronounced that no particular odour was any longer noticeable.

And then, with the soldier's help, she washed the mud-smeared sign and set off back.

But even trotting along towards the huge smooth lawns where the tea tents were, Mrs Craggs found that life inside the brick surrounding walls was still flecked in its outward smoothness by little untoward incidents. Like the policeman burrowing in the bushes.

Mrs Craggs spotted him as she was approaching a small summerhouse with a nice thatched roof to it – 'Why, I might be miles away in the country,' she had just murmured to herself – and the policeman was crouching in the bushes at the back of the building seemingly poking into a small hole below the floor level. Of course, he might have been only making certain there were no bombs under the little building. But Mrs Craggs was pretty sure he was doing nothing of the kind. She had seen too many coppers on the beat at night tucking away their packets of fags or their bits of a snack somewhere convenient to have any doubts about that.

And, just to have a little bet with herself, as soon as the constable had strolled off, looking every inch the dignified bobby – I expect they picks 'em special, Mrs Craggs thought – and perhaps adding an extra touch of stateliness by proving to have, when he could be fully seen, a magnificent and well-trimmed red beard, she trotted up to the bushes and poked her hand into the hole under the little summerhouse.

Yes, fags.

Mrs Craggs smiled. But had that thick and creamy sheet of paper stopped her telling Mrs Milhorne about this?

'Well, you've been long enough,' the tenting manager greeted her as she handed over the board. But as it was solemnly hoisted to its proper place Mrs Craggs answered not a word. Instead she went back to sweeping the floor of the huge marquee, making as good a job of it as she knew how.

But, though she was a great believer in a spot of hard work helping you to make up your mind about any problem, big or small, for all the care and vigour with which she wielded her broom no answer came to her about the question the surreptitious policeman had posed. She wanted to tell Mrs Milhorne – and all the more so because she knew telling her this would help her not to say anything about how one of the household corgis had defied even the best of arrangements – but she was not at all sure how far she could trust her friend.

As it happened, her mind was made up for her in quite a different way.

She had barely coaxed the last grains of dust from the floor into her dustpan when from just the other side of the marquee's canvas there came a yell of such volume and excruciating pain that everybody inside was frozen into stillness. Mrs Craggs, indeed, was the first to come to life. She rose from her knees, caught hold of the edge of a join in the canvas close beside her and with one heave opened a good big aperture in the tent's side.

And there, plain for all to see, was the very same red-bearded constable Mrs Craggs had been thinking of when the terrible yell had so startled them all. And, plain cause of the yell, there with its stout little jaws firmly clamped on to the blue of the policeman's trousers was the same little corgi who had already once this morning committed an outrage, on the guardsman's bearskin.

'Why, you –' shouted Mrs Craggs.

And, at the sound of that by now familiar voice, once again the little dog vanished from sight.

Which, since it was soon evident that the heavy cloth of the constable's trousers was still intact despite the corgi's best efforts, should have been the end of the incident. And it would have been, except for the constable's red beard.

Because for once at least popular belief proved true, and it turned out that the red-bearded policeman had a flaming temper. And, worse than that, it turned out his innermost political beliefs were of a rousing red character to match both temper and beard.

Terrible penalties were going to be exacted from the supposed owner of the offending canine. And the whole Press of the free world was, a trifle illogically perhaps and certainly in defiance of any papers signed, going to be enlisted in the cause of proclaiming the crime to the skies. It would have quite spoiled the garden party. Except that Mrs Craggs found an opportunity before very long to have a quiet word in the enraged ear above the flaming beard. The phrases 'little thatched hut, ever so pretty' and 'packet o' fags and who's to blame?' might have been heard, and then all of a sudden the red-bearded policeman was the soul of sweetness and the incident of the incisive corgi no more than a passing joke.

And the garden party, far from being spoiled, was a great success. The sun shone. The guests glittered. The tea was excellent, the cakes more than excellent. The bands were of a jolly oompahness not to be beaten and the hostess gracious beyond belief, if perhaps as some observers noted – Mrs Craggs from behind a cloud of fragrant steamy washing-up water among them – looking occasionally just a little tired and in need of a few moments' respite as though she had spent unexpectedly a number of frustrating and ill-spared minutes early in the day engaged in some slightly unpleasant duty like calling and calling in vain to a particularly recalcitrant pet dog, or something of that sort. But this was less than a little cloud to mar the universal joy.

Something which could not have been said of the discovery that Mrs Craggs learned of towards the end of the affair, though not so near it that the matter could be safely ignored. It was her friend of earlier in the day, the guardsman with the miraculously deodorised bearskin, who told her about it.

She had her head down in her washing-up bowl when a sudden hissing voice penetrated her cloud of steam.

'Hey, missus, he's done it again.'

She looked up, recognised her friend and therefore knew at once who 'he' was.

'That bleeding little corgi?' she said. 'What now?'

'Worse than anything. Worse than my bearskin, worse than that copper's leg, silly idiot.'

'What? What's the little perisher done? Don't jabber, lad. Speak up.'

'It's a flamingo. One of them special flamingoes, given her by the Indian Ambassador or something. It was part of my orders to keep a particular eye on them.'

'Bitten one o' them, has he?'

'Worse.'

Mrs Craggs thought like a spin-dryer.

'The corpse,' she said, reaching to the heart of the matter at once. 'Where's the corpse? If any o' the guests …'

'That's it, that's just it. It's down by the lake there. Got it round its neck when it was dipping in for a drink. And I can't think of no way of doing anything about it.'

'You wouldn't,' said Mrs Craggs, with scorn.

And she set herself to meet the challenge as she had set herself to meet any challenge that had come along in the course of a longish old life not without its crises.

It took her hardly any time, not long enough for her washing-up water to have cooled even.

Then she removed her hands from the bowl, gave them a good wipe on the edge of her flowered apron and turned to go.

'Come on,' she said to the soldier.

'Where to?'

'To get the body, o' course.'

'But what'll we do with it?'

'Hide it, lad. What else?'

'But where? Where?'

'Where the policeman hid his fags, boy. Under the floor o' that nice little thatched summerhouse they got.'

'Yeah,' said the guardsman, enlightenment dawning. 'Yeah, I know it. Seen it when I was patrolling. Yeah, just the place. Only …'

'Only what, lad? Speak up.'

'Only, well, the niff like.'

'From the body? You're right about that, lad, but you ought to know what we can do there.'

'What, then?' The guardsman had as much faith in Mrs Craggs by now as he had in his regimental sergeant-major.

'Easy, lad. Devil's Snitchbane. Much as we can grab of it.'

Mrs Craggs carried the feet and the guardsman the snake-like and drooping neck, Mrs Craggs considering that this was no less than a soldier should do. It did not take them as much as two minutes to hurry with their unseeable burden round to the back of the summerhouse, seizing on the way three stout branches from the fast diminishing clump of Snitchbane. And, though in among the bushes some difficulties presented themselves largely to do with the size of the hole in the boards, their task was all but finished inside a six-minute limit.

Until a female voice from the small curtained window

directly above coldly addressed them.

'Just what are you two doing there?'

Mrs Craggs's first thought, as she looked up from her crouching position, was that there was no way in which, on her knees, she could make even an attempt at a curtsey. Then she thought of all the circumstances that had brought about this unexpected meeting. Next, for half an instant she remembered Mrs Milhorne and the creamy sheet of paper. And finally a favourite old saying of hers planted itself firmly above the temporary confusion in her mind. 'When there ain't no 'elp fer it, there ain't nothing like the plain old truth.'

So she told it.

'But I never thought as how you'd be in there, ma'am, straight I didn't,' she concluded.

'I use it to come and freshen up if things get a bit too hectic out there,' the owner of the house (and gardens) said.

'Well, an' if I had any idea I wouldn't never have dreamt o' stuffing that old bird underneath,' Mrs Craggs replied. 'I'm right sorry, ma'am, that I am.'

'No,' said the lady of the house. 'No need to be sorry at all. The last thing any of us wants is for what little Joey has done to get out. So the sooner we all forget all about it the better, isn't it?'

'Well, yes,' said Mrs Craggs. And she was so surprised and delighted by the suggestion that she added: 'Yes, it bloody well is.'

But she did not forget about it, not for as long as she lived, though she never ever gave a solitary soul so much as a hint of it all. Mrs Craggs knows how to keep a secret, pieces of creamy paper or no pieces of creamy paper.

Mrs Milhorne. Mrs Milhorne. Just a minute.

Yaiss?

Mrs Milhorne, something I've been told I must get. It's people who've employed Mrs Craggs in their homes. Can you give me any names? I mean, of people who've employed you both, of course.

Oh, well, yaiss. We have wor – assisted in what you might call domestic homes in London as well as in places more sort of public like. Good-class 'omes, homes, always o' course.

Good. Marvellous. So could you just give me some names?

Well, actually … Well, there's not many I can give. I mean, when it's a 'ome, home, Mrs Craggs'd be working there on her own, wouldn't she? The people are not likely to want me to assist as well, are they?

So you can't actually give me any names, of Mrs Craggs's private employers?

Well, there was the person she was working for later on when she had that job first thing in the morning at the Halbert Hall, the Royal Halbert Hall I should say. Only that sort of ended in, well, what you might call tragedy, reely. Tragedy all round, I'd say.

VI

MRS CRAGGS AND THE LATE PRINCE ALBERT

WHEN MRS CRAGGS USED TO clean the Royal Albert Hall, or
to be strictly accurate several offices within it, it was her habit
leaving in the early morning, her work thoroughly done, to
walk through the Park to her second job of the day. Almost
every time she did so she lingered at the Albert Memorial,
climbing its many shallow steps and wandering round looking
at all its myriad statues, the groups representing the Four
Continents, the labelled groups representing the four pillars of
prosperity; Agriculture, Manufacture, Commerce and Engi-
neering, and the long four-sided panel of great men – a
hundred and sixty-nine of them, she had counted – running all
round the base.

She liked them all, the statues, though she had her favourites
and her less favoured. A lot of effort had been put into making
them and setting them round the great edifice which enshrouds
the high tiny representation of the Consort himself, Albert the
Good. She liked Albert, too. If by all he had done in life he had
earned such mighty works as the Memorial and the massy
circular Albert Hall, then, she thought, he must have been a
hard worker too. And she honoured him for that.

So it was a matter of bitter regret to her for years and years
that it was through her fault that bloody murder occurred one

morning on the very steps leading up to the great man's memorial.

It came about in this way. Every day as she made her tour of honour she used to see an odd trio of people hold a short meeting at the foot of the steps below. Two of them were identically track-suited joggers and the third was a shortish, bald-headed man dressed invariably in overalls. The joggers would run up and wait, panting a little, till the man in overalls came walking up from the roadway, and then they would all three have some conversation, always very businesslike, usually quite brief, just sometimes more lengthy.

From the start their talk looked as though it was meant to be secret. But there was seldom anyone else nearby at that hour and somehow the three of them, having seen Mrs Craggs every day, soon discounted her presence and spoke quite loudly. In this way she got to know a good deal about the three and about the subject of their mysterious meetings.

The two joggers, she learnt, were brothers, a pair of lookalikes if ever there was. She even eventually got to know their names, Allingham and Bellingham Smith. Mr Allingham and Mr Bellingham, the third individual, whom Mrs Craggs knew only as the Technician, called them. Bel and Al they usually called each other.

Except for the occasions when Bellingham, who was quick and alert as the grey squirrels that scampered on the Park paths nearby, called his brother in exasperation 'Albert'.

'Albert the Good, Albert the Dull,' Mrs Craggs heard him say once. And didn't like him any the better for it.

The subject of the clandestine meetings, Mrs Craggs bit by bit got to know, was something called the Heart Perpetuator. It seemed to be, as far as she could make out, a tiny thing you would wear clamped to your ribs which would not only keep an eye, or an ear, on your heart to detect the least earliest sign of anything going wrong but would also send little waves of something or other through your body that would at once put the trouble right.

The two brothers, who were scientists at Imperial College

just down the road, were inventing it as a secret, out-of-hours project and the Technician was – their technician.

He was, in fact, the one who combined the different contributions of each brother – Bel had the brilliant ideas; Al was the one who got there by sheer hard thinking – into something real and solid, the prototype, as they called it when at last the whole secret enterprise neared completion.

In the long months while the device gradually approached this state, not without setbacks and dramas (these last particularly from the effervescent Bellingham), Mrs Craggs had grown extremely interested in the heart perpetuator. And this was what led in the end to murder.

Because all unwittingly one late morning at her second job, cleaning a very posh flat in Mayfair, she mentioned the magical machine to her employer. It was something to chat about, something she thought interesting. But to her surprise next day her employer's husband, a gentleman she had never seen before, questioned her closely about what she knew. She thought no more of it afterwards, except to reflect that some people had more time on their hands than they knew what to do with. And it was only a fortnight or so later, when she witnessed the terrific quarrel that broke out at the dawn meeting on the Memorial steps, that she realised, with a horrible sinking feeling, just what she had done.

The quarrel was, she understood in a moment, about a proposal by the Technician to leave Imperial College and go to the great multi-national, Inter-Colloids, where as a newly made director of research he would set up a whole division to manufacture heart perpetuators, to be sold at a very high price to millionaires, oil sheikhs and captains of industry.

Mrs Craggs was outraged at the use that had been made of her. But the rest of the quarrel on the steps below was so interesting that she had to postpone thinking about that till some more convenient time.

The two brothers were each equally furious with the Technician. Darting Bellingham was enraged because he had seen the three of them setting up on their own much such a firm as the new division of Inter-Colloids. The sober, even dull, Allingham was angry because it had been his idea that they would simply send details of what they had perfected to something called 'the journals'. Mrs Craggs wasn't certain what these were, but she thought Allingham, Albert the Good, was right.

At that moment, however, sharp-eyed, squirrel-alert Bellingham spotted her and the three of them dropped into fierce undertones to continue their dispute.

And the next day the Technician was murdered.

Mrs Craggs saw it happen. Apparently he had arrived at the morning trysting-place a little earlier than usual, before she had got to the Memorial herself. But he had been met not by both brothers jogging up to him but by one of them only. At a distance Mrs Craggs could not be sure which. But she could see quite clearly what it was he did.

He pulled a short sort of club from his track-suit trousers and with a single blow to the Technician's bare bald head felled him to the ground beside the Memorial's knobbed and spiked railing.

Mrs Craggs yelled out. She couldn't help it, although she was much too far away to be able to do anything. However, her single shocked cry must have been heard by the murderer because he looked round, saw her beginning to trundle forward at a run and took to his heels.

Of course, she couldn't possibly catch him. There were thirty years and more in age between them. So when she got to where the Technician lay she stopped, made sure that he was indeed dead and then went for a policeman.

There wasn't much she could say when she found a passing copper. But she had the satisfaction of thinking that she had at least alerted the forces of law and order as quickly as could be, and she trusted that they would do the rest.

It turned out her trust was not exactly rewarded.

Later that morning, in the posh Mayfair flat, she learnt that a detective chief inspector wanted to see her. He proved to be a man she took against almost straight away. It was only because, heavily moustached and sullenly determined, his face reminded her at once of the rifle-carrying Plainsman from the Memorial group symbolising 'America', one of her least favourite of all the statues. She did her best to suppress the feeling. But she wasn't very successful.

Especially when Detective Chief Inspector America went on and on trying to make her say which of the brothers it was that she had seen. Right from the start she'd told him she couldn't at that distance tell one from the other. But he would go on. Just like, she thought, one of the Park squirrels with a specially hard nut to crack.

At last, acknowledging her stone-wall refusal, he came out with what was the real source of his trouble.

'You see, this is what we call a premeditated affair,' he said, explaining with heavy patience. 'The weapon, that little club you saw, had actually been fashioned as an exact replica of one of the knobs on the Memorial railing. Given a minute or two more, our man would have nicely set up the death as some sort of curious accident. But, by the time we'd discovered where the brothers lived, in separate nearby flats as a matter of fact, first we found Mr Bellingham Smith still in bed and drugged to the wide – had to break in, tell the truth – then, when we went to Mr Allingham Smith's, it turned out to be exactly the same with him.'

Mrs Craggs looked unbelieving.

'Well, of course,' Detective Chief Inspector America went on, 'one of them was faking it, one had doped his brother and gone off and done the murder and then had come back and doped himself. But – keep this to yourself, mind – we're damned if we can tell which. Not the officers who saw them first, not the police surgeon. Not me.'

The outraged squeak with which he delivered these last two words from behind his thickly curving moustaches put Mrs Craggs in the picture straight away. Unless Chief Inspector America could sort out which of the two brothers had used that deadly cosh and which one had, innocently drugged, slept through the whole time of the crime, he would be unable to make an arrest.

She thought for a second or two, eyes tight closed.

Then she told the grimly determined chief inspector what he wanted to hear.

'You know which of 'em it really was, don't you?' she said, though she was perfectly well aware that he was thoroughly stumped.

Chief Inspector America remained silent. But slowly above his ponderous moustaches his cheeks went a dull red.

'Supposing you – er – give me your opinion,' he said at last.

'It's not opinion,' Mrs Craggs answered. 'It's plain downright fact.'

'Your fact then. If you'd be so good.'

'Albert,' said Mrs Craggs then, with a long, long sigh. 'It was Albert the Good, Albert the Dull.'

'Albert? But neither of them's called –'

'Oh, Allingham then, if you must have it all correct.'

'Allingham? But why? From what I've heard from you and others Bellingham's the one with the brains.'

'Not a bit of it. My Albert the Good's every bit as high-powered in the brain-box department. It's just that he's the painstaking one. The one that's got to get everything right before he settles for it. If it'd been Bellingham what done the murder, he'd have just killed that nasty greedy man and then tried to talk his way out of it afterwards.'

'Well,' said Chief Inspector America, 'it's true we did find a phial of a highly toxic chemical Bellingham apparently had misappropriated from Imperial College when we searched his flat. And we were thinking of arresting him on the strength of that, if you couldn't come up with a proper identification.'

He put a large red hand up in front of his moustache and coughed.

'I suppose in view of what you've just disclosed you wouldn't care to identify Allingham Smith now?' he asked.

'I would not,' said Mrs Craggs.

'No, I thought you wouldn't. So what am I to do? What you've told me isn't what we in the police call good evidence, you know.'

'No, I suppose it ain't,' Mrs Craggs said. 'So now you want to know how you can pin it fair and square on poor old Albert?'

'Yes,' said Chief Inspector America quite simply.

So Mrs Craggs told him.

And, of course, when the chief inspector pretended to arrest the brilliant Bellingham, Allingham, Albert the Good, Albert the Dull, promptly confessed.

Yes. And there's something else, Mrs Milhorne.

Always willing to oblige. I mean, if it's the television.

Good. Well, it's like this. We always like on 'This Is' to have a bit of sloppy stuff, you know. A first sweetheart, something of that sort. It goes down well with the live audience. So, do you happen to know if Mrs Craggs had something going with someone when she was still a girl? Especially if he's in, say, Australia now and we could fly him over?

Well, no. No, I don't see old Elma having what you might call a real romance. Now, if it was me you were wanting on the programme …

No. No, I'm afraid that's out of the question.

Well, please yourself. But I can't tell you anything about any sweethearts for Mrs Craggs. No. Not but what she ain't got her softer side. Underneath it all.

Oh, yes? Tell me. That might make …

Well, I'm thinking about the time we was assisting in Berkeley Square. Very nice class o' people, though I don't know as I reely believe it about that nightingale. I mean, Elma Craggs must of made that up. It's more the sort o' thing you'd expect from one o' them story writers, if you ask me.

VII

Mrs Craggs Hears the Nightingale

Pom Pom pom-pom Pom-pom-pom Pom, and a Nightingale sang in Berkeley Squaaare.

'I dare say it did, dear,' Mrs Craggs said from down on her knees swabbing the kitchen floor of the prestige offices of the Zinc Development Association, Berkeley Square, London W1, where she and Mrs Milhorne were beginning their afternoon tasks. 'I dare say it did, but it never made no noise like you.'

Mrs Milhorne abruptly halted the sweeping slow foxtrot she had been performing in accompaniment to the music still in her head.

'I got a very nice voice,' she said. 'My rendition o' that song was what first drew Milhorne's attention. A lovely voice, he told me. Small, but lovely.'

Mrs Craggs forbore to ask whether it was that voice remaining small but ceasing to be lovely which had been responsible for any of the never mentioned departures of Mr Milhorne. After all, she and Mrs Milhorne were friends, had been for years, and it wasn't fair to try friendship too far, truth or no truth.

Instead she gave a final swish of the cloth to her floor, rose to her feet, swilled out the cloth in the sink and began to take out of the big cupboard all the teacups and saucers which at half-past three exactly two pretty tea-girls would take round to the various offices in the building together with two chocolate digestive biscuits, just as at eleven in the morning precisely they had taken round coffee, together with two plain Petit Beurre biscuits.

Mrs Milhorne did not give Mrs Craggs any help. She was instead standing by the narrow window of the kitchen, looking down on the big tree-shaded expanse of Berkeley Square itself.

'Yaiss,' she said after a little. 'Yaiss, he's edging nearer. He's edging nearer. I said he would, and he has. He's edged a whole lot nearer.'

'Who's edged nearer what?' Mrs Craggs said. 'Half-past three's edging a whole lot nearer us, I do know. An' them old Zincs'll be wanting their teas.'

Mrs Milhorne ignored the second part of Mrs Craggs's remark and leant her bony frame a few inches further out of the window.

'Oh,' she said dreamily, 'I do like to see it. I do like to see young love.'

'That,' said Mrs Craggs. 'I might have guessed it.'

'Well, what's wrong with young love?' Mrs Milhorne demanded, withdrawing from the window.

'Oh, there's nothing wrong with a bit o' love,' Mrs Craggs said. 'Provided it's at the right time an' in the right place. But Berkeley Square coming up to tea time ain't the right place and it ain't the right time.'

'You and your teacups,' Mrs Milhorne answered, making a vague move in the direction of the chocolate digestives which she was accustomed to place on the cups' saucers in a way that she clearly considered showed great artistic skill.

'Anyhow,' she said, 'I think it's her lunch hour. I think she gets her lunch hour late. I seen her before.'

'Oh, yes,' Mrs Craggs said, 'an' she don't eat a speck o' lunch either, but goes moonin' about with some young feller, I know.'

'No, you don't. First time she's met him.'

Mrs Milhorne thrust yoke-thin shoulders out of the window once more.

'Oh, yaiss,' she said. 'They're talking now. Talking and sitting ever so close.'

She manoeuvred herself back in and gave a long deep sigh, mostly over the packet of chocolate digestives she had just opened.

'The first meeting,' she said. 'I remember it was just the same meself. Edging.'

'I thought he come up and said you'd got a lovely voice, but small.'

'That was Milhorne. That was later. Milhorne weren't the first. I was the belle o' many a ball, I was. In my day.'

Mrs Craggs, carrying a tower of cups round to the second tea trolley, glanced out of the open window. She had no difficulty in seeing the young man and the girl Mrs Milhorne had been giving her running commentary on. They were sitting on a bench inside the Square underneath one of the huge spreading plane trees whose branches cascaded delicately down in the soft spring air. She was pretty, no doubt about that. Pretty as a picture, Mrs Craggs thought, with her neat head of swinging blonde hair and her crisp pink-and-white candy-stripe dress with the white cardigan just thrown across her shoulders. Just the way I was meself once upon a time.

Or, no, she acknowledged, the lass down there's something out of the ordinary. Prettier than a picture. He's a lucky lad if he's getting off with her.

She paused a moment longer to give the young man a rigorous inspection. And was not altogether sure whether he came out of it well or not. He looked all right. In some ways. He was tall and had a good pair of shoulders on him. Too much hair, of course. But most of them had that nowadays. Still, he looked nice and clean, and bursting with health too.

But those clothes. A pair of jeans all ragged at the bottoms. A pullover with frayed sleeve-ends. And, if she wasn't mistaken, a shirt collar that was as worn as her old piece of swabbing rag.

A girl as pretty as that deserved something better. And what was that he had on the bench beside him? A violin case, it looked like. A battered old violin case. What was a young man doing carrying round a violin case? Full of bombs, likely as not.

'Ain't they a lovely pair?' Mrs Milhorne's voice came from behind her. '*Pom* pom *Pom*-pom *Pom*-pom-pom *Pom*, and a Nightingale sang in Berkeley Square.'

Mrs Craggs put down her tower of teacups with a sharp clatter.

'Be some o' those Zincs singing another tune altogether in Berkeley Square in a minute,' she said.

Mrs Milhorne hurriedly dabbed chocolate digestives by the pair on saucer after saucer.

'Yeah,' she said. 'It's a pity though that nightingales don't sing in the day, otherwise one might sing for the two o' them now. Lovely, it'd be.'

Mrs Craggs snorted.

'Nightingales not sing in the day,' she said. 'Lot o' nonsense. If you'd been brought up in the country like what I was, you'd know better. Nightingales sing just when they wants, an' good luck to 'em. Though I don't suppose it's very likely as you'd get one singing here in Berkeley Square no more, not now.'

'No,' Mrs Milhorne agreed. 'All this environment. They've all gone, the birds have. All gone.'

''Cept the pigeons,' said Mrs Craggs. 'Dirty beasts.'

* * *

In the days and weeks that followed, Mrs Craggs and Mrs Milhorne saw a good deal of the two young people who had met under the big plane tree in the Square that time. Even the very next day it was clear that the talk the young man with the battered violin case had succeeded in having with the more than pretty girl with the neatly swinging blonde hair had been the beginning of something. For one thing, Mrs Milhorne spotted him waiting for her long before her lunch hour was due. 'I expect she's a secretary kept late,' Mrs Milhorne said. 'Managing director's secretary, that's what she'll be, pretty as that.' And for another thing, as soon as the girl did appear she made straight for the very same bench under the delicately cascading plane tree, and the smile she gave when she realised he was there was plain to see even from right across the busy roadway.

The day afterwards when the two of them sat together on the bench it was with his arm round her shoulders straight away, and you could see, despite all the roar and racket of the traffic, that they were talking together and laughing together nineteen to the dozen.

Some time during the second week of it Mrs Craggs made a small discovery, one which she did not lose much time in passing on to her fellow worker.

'Secretary you said, managing director's secretary, weren't it?' she murmured over Mrs Milhorne's bony shoulder as the latter leant out of the window to look at the pair of them once more, her long pale face moony as if a nightingale really was singing out there instead of the traffic jostling and snarling.

'Yaiss,' Mrs Milhorne answered absently. 'Bound to be a top secretary. When you're as pretty as that, you get the job to go with it. I was thinking o' being a secretary once. Only I couldn't learn the shorthand, not with me nerves the way they've always been.'

'Saw her coming out o' her place o' work this morning,' Mrs Craggs said.

'Oooh, did you? Where was it? That big car showroom over the way? Or was it the posh flower shop. She might be an assistant there instead. Assistant going on to be manageress when she's a bit older. Yaiss, I like that. A pretty face among all them pretty flowers.'

'Chambermaid,' said Mrs Craggs.

Mrs Milhorne dropped a chocolate digestive and it shattered to fragments on the floor.

'Yes,' said Mrs Craggs. 'I was passing that big hotel just down beyond the far corner of the square there this morning and out she come.'

'Well, that don't mean nothing. I expect she's the manager's secretary there. All among them rich guests an' all.'

'Come out talking to another girl,' said Mrs Craggs. 'Talking about making beds and cleaning baths they was. Her name's Patty by the way. Patty.'

Mrs Milhorne put some more chocolate digestives on saucers with less than her customary artistic finesse.

'Well,' she said, after a while, 'it don't make him any less keen on Patty, her being that.'

'Being what?' Mrs Craggs asked, a little wickedly.

'Being what you said.'

* * *

It was true enough. If the boy with the violin case did know what Patty did for a living – and from the way they talked to each other all the time when they met, talked and talked and laughed and laughed, it was pretty well certain to Mrs Craggs and Mrs Milhorne that she had told him everything about herself from the day she was born onwards – it clearly made no difference to him. Even Mrs Craggs had to acknowledge that she had never seen two such lovebirds as the pair of them every day as they sat there under the big cascading plane tree.

She wondered sometimes, however, about how much to do with himself he might have told Patty. It was the violin case that chiefly worried her. The boy always had it with him, but he never opened it. And Mrs Craggs couldn't quite get out of her mind the thought of bombs or something else nasty every time she saw it.

Until one day.

It was an afternoon that was, for some reason, rather quieter than usual on the roads round the square. The traffic, for once, was not racketing and jostling but flowed smoothly and easily. There was even a fashion photographer at work in the spring sunshine just outside the square's railings there, making a tall statuesque model walk up and down on the pavement and snapping her time and again against the background of the peaceful gardens. ('I was going in for a model once,' Mrs Milhorne remarked.)

And suddenly, as Mrs Craggs and Mrs Milhorne watched, the boy did open the battered old case, and in it there wasn't the trace of a bomb or of anything else but what a violin case should have in it, a violin. The boy lifted the instrument out of the old case with delicate care and put it to his shoulder. And then he began to play. To play to Patty.

The sound of the melody – it was a love song, clearly a love song even if neither Mrs Craggs nor Mrs Milhorne could put a single word to it – floated up to them above the quiet whirring of the cars and taxis circling the square, sweet and rounded and true, and before very many moments has passed Mrs Milhorne was wiping the tears from her long pale face and even Mrs Craggs was constrained to give a quiet sniff.

'I know what he is now,' Mrs Milhorne said. 'He's one o' them great violinists. I bet he plays every day at that Wigmore Hall place on the other side of Oxford Street. I bet he does.'

But that afternoon, going home by Tube for a change, Mrs Craggs discovered that once more her friend was labouring under a misapprehension. She decided next morning, when they arrived to do their early office-cleaning stint, that it would be kinder to break the news before Mrs Milhorne found out for herself. 'He's no great violinist, I'm afraid,' she said.

Mrs Milhorne bridled.

'Well, what is he then?' she demanded. 'I s'pose you're going to say he's a hotel waiter next.'

'Worse,' said Mrs Craggs. 'Hotel waiter's a steady job. And respectable.'

'Well, what's he do that's not respectable? An' Patty so pretty she deserves a hotel manager, never mind waiter.'

'Busker,' said Mrs Craggs. 'There he was just inside the tunnel into Bond Street Tube. Playing away on that old fiddle of his. What they call "country" now, I think, though it's not the country I was brought up in. Silly American stuff.'

'Perhaps he was just practising there,' Mrs Milhorne suggested.

Mrs Craggs gave a rich snort.

'With a cap full o' pennies, an' ten pences too, there in front of him? Be your age.'

That afternoon the traffic round the square was back to its normal grinding and jerking racket and the boy's violin did not come out of its battered old case to sing its strangely sweet love song. Mrs Craggs was quite glad of that: she felt it would be a bit cruel on her friend to be reminded of that shattered dream of the concert violinist and the humble chambermaid.

And a day or two later she got to learn that Mrs Milhorne was not the only one to be disappointed over what the boy did in order to make ends meet. The first sign of trouble came during her own lunch break. She had gone out with Mrs Milhorne and taken sandwiches and the evening paper into the square gardens because it was an even nicer sunny day. Suddenly Mrs Milhorne, who had been chatting away loudly enough about her nerves, broke off and thrust her face close to Mrs Craggs's ear.

'It's her,' she whispered, in a draught like the back-end of a vacuum-cleaner. 'It's her. Patty.'

Mrs Craggs looked round.

Patty had evidently been away from the hotel just past the far corner of the square on some quick errand or other, and she was now hurrying back. But on that wonderfully pretty face beneath the swing of neat blonde hair there was something more than a look of simple intent to get back to work as rapidly as possibly. There was an expression of puzzlement. And more than a hint of anger, too. Had she passed by the side entrance to Bond Street Underground station and seen someone there, someone making a living by busking?

Mrs Craggs made a point of getting well ahead with her preparations for tea for 'them Zincs' when they got back so as to be able to devote more than her usual time to looking down at the lovebirds under the big spreading plane tree. She had a feeling that all was not going to be as full of laughter and sweet looks as it generally was.

She was right, too.

No sooner had Patty arrived at the bench where the boy with the battered old violin case was waiting for her than she exploded. Up above and with all the noisy cars in between, Mrs Craggs and Mrs Milhorne could not of course hear a word that was said. But they hardly needed to. It was perfectly plain that Patty was bawling the boy out, up hill and down dale. And from the way her finger darted out and pointed like a shaft of fury at the violin case it was clear that this was indeed the seat of trouble.

The boy plainly tried protesting, but it was clear that he must in fact have been deceiving Patty all along about what it was that he did. And she was not going to put up with it.

'Quite right, too,' said Mrs Craggs.

'But they were so much in love,' wailed Mrs Milhorne.

'Well, if he really loves her, he'll do something about it still. He'll get himself a proper job and let her know he has. Why, he could go down the street to that hotel and get himself taken on there. Kitchen porter. Anything. But some respectable way of earning a living. And then he'd be sure to bump into her there, and things'd be as right as rain in two twos.'

Mrs Milhorne sighed.

'Oh, it'd be lovely. Lovely.'

But it quite soon began to look as if it never would be lovely at all. First, Patty wheeled round and marched off back towards the hotel – 'an' she's not had a bite of their rolls,' Mrs Milhorne moaned – and then something altogether worse happened. Two police constables, who had been parading slowly past the square railings, suddenly began to hurry, almost ran round to the gate, went in and went straight across to the plane tree where the boy with the violin case was sitting stupefied on the bench. At once they began to question him, and soon it was clear that they were not being too polite about it.

'What's he done?' asked Mrs Milhorne. 'Whatever has he done?'

'I know what they think he's done,' Mrs Craggs said.

And she pulled from her sagging shopping-bag her evening

paper and pointed a lean finger at its banner headlines.

THE STOLEN STRAD. *Wigmore Hall Theft From Maestro*

A moment later it looked as though her guess was right. The policeman made the boy open his old violin case and then, despite his evident protests, they lifted the instrument from it and pointed out eagerly to each other some marks on the back.

'But he had that violin long before the Strad was stolen,' Mrs Milhorne said. 'Or ... or ... oh, dear.'

A look of complete dismay came on to her face.

'Yaiss,' she said at last. 'Yaiss, that'll be it. He stole the Strad from the Wigmore Hall, threw away his own rotten old fiddle and put the stolen one in the case instead. Why, the dirty devil. I always knew he wasn't what he seemed. Said it a hundred times, didn't I?'

'No,' said Mrs Craggs, 'you didn't.'

Down below in the square the two policemen were hustling the boy away.

Mrs Craggs looked at them. And before they had quite got out of sight, heading in the direction of the police station at Vine Street, a look of determination came on to her creased and lined nut-brown face.

'Yeh,' she said. 'Yeh.'

She snatched her hat from the peg on the kitchen door and crammed it back on to her head.

'You'll have to see to them Zincs' tea on your own today,' she said to Mrs Milhorne. 'I got business to attend to.'

And, without another word, she hurried down to the ground floor of the glittering prestige office building and out into the square.

*　*　*

Mrs Milhorne was late for work next morning. Almost an hour late.

'It was the News,' she explained to Mrs Craggs when at last she did arrive. 'I kept waiting to hear the News to see if they'd got anything on it about the boy and the violin. There wasn't nothing in the paper, and you'd of thought there would be after all the fuss they made yesterday. I mean "Stolen Strad Arrest", that'd be news, wouldn't it?'

'It would be,' said Mrs Craggs. 'If there'd been any arrest.'

'What you mean? We saw 'em, didn't we? Saw them two coppers with our own eyes.'

'But that weren't all we saw with our own eyes,' Mrs Craggs replied.

'What you mean?'

'Well, didn't we see that boy – his name's Alan, by the way, Alan Lambert, and he's the son o' that millionaire Sir Peter Lambert, only he quarrelled with him and left home – well, didn't we both see him take his violin out of his case days before that Strad was stolen. An' didn't we both hear him play it, sweet as a nightingale?'

'Well, what if we did?'

'This is what. It was plain as a pikestaff to me that the boy had got a top-notch violin in his case all along. Busking at Bond Street tube he may have been, but that was no tuppenny-ha'penny fiddle he had, not by the way he took it so gentle from its case and not by the sound he got out of it when he played.'

Mrs Milhorne did some thinking.

'So you went along to Vine Street an' told them,' she said. 'An' they believed you.'

'Not a bit of it. That's why I never came back all afternoon.'

'But what then? They've let him go, haven't they? Young Alan.'

'They let him go. When we traced that photographer.'

'What photographer? I don't remember no photographer.'

'The one taking fashion pictures that day. Just when Alan was playing to Patty. Colour pictures they were, and they showed his own violin a treat. Wasn't no arguing about it after that.'

'Cor,' said Mrs Milhorne. 'So it all ends happily after all.'

Mrs Craggs smiled then, a great big broad grin cracking her old nut of a face.

'It does end happy,' she said. 'But more than you thought. You ought to have been here at six this morning, like I was. You really did ought.'

'But why ever?'

'Because at six this morning, when it was quiet as quiet outside an' might have been right in the middle of the country, I heard the sound o' violin music. Music as sweet as any you ever listened to, right out there in the square.'

'It was him? It was Alan?'

'It was. And something more.'

'What? What ever?'

'You look out o' the window here. Look right across the square, and what do you see at the far end, past the big block o' posh flats?'

Mrs Milhorne thrust her scraggy neck as far out of the window as she could.

'Only the top of some tall building,' she said.

'A top with little windows in it?'

'Yes. There's windows.'

'Them's the windows right at the top of the big hotel there. The windows of the rooms where the maids an' that sleep. And one o' them windows opened a bit after the music started. It opened wide and someone leant out and waved. Waved and waved.'

'Patty. It was Patty.'

''Course it was. An' something more.'

'What more? There couldn't be no more, not after that.'

'There was. After the music had been going a little, I heard another sound. I swear I did.'

'What was that? What ever was that?'

Mrs Craggs looked at her friend. There was a tear in the corner of her eye.

'I heard it,' she said. 'I did. A nightingale sang in Berkeley Square.'

Mrs Milhorne, there is —

— as I was saying, sensitive Elma Craggs ain't. I say
nothink, of course. I mean, what'd be the use? But
sometimes I have to shut my ears. The things she says.
And the people she says them to. I mean, she ain't got –
she has not got – she has not received no respect for
people of what you might call respectability what she
happens to hencounter. Now, I'm quite different. I —

Mrs Milhorne. That's interesting, but there's something
important I must ask. Sometimes on 'This Is' when we go
downmarket for a change – very popular if you don't do it too
often – we find a potential Victim's just not going to be able to
stand up to it. Now, can you assure me Mrs Craggs won't go
dumb, for instance, when she sees all the cameras and lights?

Well, that's what I been saying, ain't I? Have I not? No
respect. Elma Craggs ain't going to go dumb just because
she sees the nice gentleman with the big red book, believe
you me. Why, you should hear some of the things she's
said to top Scotland Yarders, superintendents. And
commodores too, I dare say.

Well, yes, but —

Of course, sometimes I only got what she tells me to go

on. I mean, I ain't heard every word what she's ever spoken. An' sometimes I does wonder – It does hoccur to me I should say, whether everything I hear's strictly, as you might say, true. I mean, what about the names of some of them superintendents she says she's given one of her dressing-downs to? I mean, Superintendent Mouse. Ain't that the sort o' name only some silly book-writer would give to a police officer? I mean, if he was sort of beefy. For the contrast, like. Well, I mean, isn't it?

VIII

A Dangerous Thing, Mrs Craggs

A CERTAIN NUMBER OF THE cleaning jobs that Mrs Craggs had at one time or another in the sprawling conglomeration of London took her into places which it is not given to everyone to enter. Perhaps the one of these that she liked the best was the Reading Room at the British Museum.

Of course, she saw little of the Reading Room while it was properly in use, when the Readers were there deep in volumes from that huge collection to which by law every single book, magazine, fascicle or pamphlet published in Great Britain must be sent. But she liked the stately, quiet atmosphere of the huge round chamber under its shallow glass dome as she polished its great floor early in the mornings before the hour of opening. She liked the encircling shelves of leather-smelling tomes, the *British Union Catalogue of Periodicals*, the *Bibliothèque Nationale Catalogue des Imprimés*, the *Cumulative Book Index*, the *Annual Register*, the *Calendars of State Papers*, Halsbury's *Statutes of England*, *Notes and Queries* and the long run of *The Gentleman's Magazine*. And she very much liked what she saw of the learned people who began to come in at 9.30 a.m.

They might not, she would often think, be any great shakes as specimens of physical beauty, running as they did for the most part to shoulders stooped and rounded by long hours bent over volumes laid out on desks and to posteriors more adapted to the seated attitude than to the soldierly march or the elegance of the dance. But, by and large, the love of their work, the love of scholarship for the sake of scholarship, shone in their eyes, gleamed clearly through spectacle lenses often neglectfully smeared. And Mrs Craggs, though she was the first to acknowledge that she was not usually much of a reader herself, loved them for that.

Not that she loved every single one she chanced to see after her chief duty of polishing that enormous circular floor with its radiating spokes of Readers' desks was over and she was occupied in seeing to parts of the huge learning machine not open to the public, even to that privileged section of them in possession of Readers' Admission Tickets. There were a few individuals she had picked out as being, for all their industry at their desks, not proper scholars, not people dedicated to the pursuit of knowledge for its own sake. Most of these 'whizzers', as Mrs Craggs called them in her own mind, were comparatively young, though they were not all necessarily so. And she would have had difficulty, had she been asked, in saying just what it was about them that marked them out for her.

Perhaps it was the way they always hurried. They hurried to be first in the short queues waiting to hand in book application slips at the small circular area that forms the hub of the Room's great wheel. They hurried, first thing in the morning, to occupy some particular one of the 390 blue-leather-covered desks which they considered to be nearest the particular reference works on the Room's perimeter that they might need. They hurried, when Closing Time came, to be first in the queues to hand back their books for safe keeping during the night. 'Whizzers', in Mrs Craggs's eyes, spoilt the slow, quiet, studious atmosphere of the place much as a garish half-squashed Coke can spoils the beauty of some ancient close-mown lawn on to which it has been carelessly thrown.

Once she overheard one of her gentlemen, one of the ones who was certainly not a whizzer, quoting a couple of lines of poetry to himself as he toddled away to get some lunch at midday

'A little learning is a dang'rous thing;
Drink deep, or taste not the Pierian spring.'

She had often wondered what the heck a Pierian spring was, but she had had no difficulty in at once agreeing with the bit about 'a little learning'. It was a dangerous thing, she knew that in her bones. And it was the whizzers who had it, and would be dangerous some day to someone somewhere.

Before long there came a time when she had startling proof of this. It was on a day that began no differently from any other. Except for one funny thing.

Mrs Craggs had been standing at the entrance to the Reading Room in the lofty inner hall of the vast Museum itself, talking to a friend of hers, one of the warders who check people going in to make sure they are in possession of a Reader's Ticket. It was a slack time, shortly after the first small rush of Readers when the Museum opens, and Mr Meiklejohn, a Scot who had lost none of his Scottishness for long residence in London, had been glad of a few moments' chat. They had just got on to the subject of whizzers, though Mrs Craggs was keeping her pet name for them to herself, and Mr Meiklejohn, who was a pretty formidable scholar himself – if the faces of Readers, past, present, long-term and temporary, is a subject for scholarship – was agreeing that there were 'bodies you can pick out who are never your regular Reader the way a Reader ought tae be', when a very, very elderly man came slowly, slowly up to the entrance.

He looked, thought Mrs Craggs, about as old as anybody could be. He had a little stooped frail body that shuffled forwards under an enormous old overcoat, despite the summer heat, like a tortoise in its shell. His head, on which a few white hairs were spread this way and that, poked out on the end of a scrawny, thin length of neck round which an old grey woollen muffler was wrapped. And he surveyed the world cautiously through a pair of tiny glinting pince-nez spectacles.

123

Mr Meiklejohn stepped forward and asked with grave Scottish courtesy if he could see his Reader's Ticket.

'Reader's Ticket?' said the old gentleman, as if such an object were something he had once heard of, dimly. 'Reader's Ticket? Well, yes, I suppose I have a Reader's Ticket. Must have been given one when I first used the Library, in '99, I think that must have been. Ninety-nine or '98, can't quite remember.'

Mr Meiklejohn shot Mrs Craggs a quick glance of amazement. Could the old boy really be meaning that he had first come to the Reading Room in the year 1899, or even 1898, eighty years ago? Was it possible?

And Mrs Craggs, looking at that peering scaly tortoise head on its long thin desiccated scarf-wound neck, thought that, well, it might be. It might really be. It would make the old boy probably a hundred years old, a bit less if he had begun to come to the Reading Room as a bright lad of eighteen or nineteen, but anyhow within a few months of his century. And he looked old enough to be a centenarian, every bit.

'Have you got your Ticket on you now, sir?' Mr Meiklejohn asked, pitching his voice a wee bit loudly in case the old gentleman was hard of hearing.

'On me? Now? I might have. I suppose I might have. Somewhere. But why on earth do you want to know?'

Mr Meiklejohn strove not to allow too astonished a look to appear on his features.

'We have to examine Reader's Tickets now, sir,' he said. 'It's a Regulation. Has been for – for a good many years, sir.'

'Oh. Oh, I see. Unauthorised fellers trying to make their way inside, eh?'

'Something like that, sir. And there have been thefts, sir, I'm sorry to say.'

'Thefts? Thefts, eh? What is the world coming to when a scholar and gentleman will steal from his own Library?'

'Aye, it's a terrible thing, sir. A terrible thing. But I'm afraid it means I'll have to see your Ticket, sir.'

'Oh, of course. Of course.'

124

The old gentleman brought one rather trembly grey-woollen-gloved hand to join the other and with extreme slowness plucked off the right-hand glove. He then seemed in some doubt about what to do with it.

'Might I hold that for you, sir?' asked Mr Meiklejohn.

'Oh. Oh, yes. Yes. Good of you.'

Mr Meiklejohn secured the grey glove – the tips of its fingers had been carefully darned once, many years ago – and the old gentleman plunged his free hand into the recesses of his overcoat.

A sudden rattling noise, like a quick burst of fire from a Uzi sub-machine gun, came from just behind them. Mrs Craggs and Mr Meiklejohn looked round. It was a Reader, a Reader wanting to enter and coughing to draw attention to his need. And, in that one quick, half-second glance, Mrs Craggs put him down at once as a whizzer, a whizzer plainly in a fury because he was being held up from plunging into the Reading Room and his waiting books.

'One moment, if you please, Mr Tipton-Martin,' said Mr Meiklejohn, authority on Readers' faces.

Mr Tipton-Martin, who was about twenty-four or twenty-five, with a pale, slightly fat face and pale, well-brushed hair, wearing not the neglected clothes that most Readers seemed to possess but a well-pressed light blue safari suit with a shirt in broad blue and white stripes to match, gave Mr Meiklejohn a glance of suppressed rage. But there was nothing he could do about getting through the narrow entrance to the Reading Room before the old gentleman.

For perhaps as much as a minute or more the latter fished waveringly inside his overcoat. But then his hand emerged gripping a time-polished leather wallet. With trembling fingers, rather hampered by the grey glove still on his other hand, he attempted to pull out from it a small card that once might have been white but was now grey with age.

'Should I give you a hand, sir?' asked Mr Meiklejohn.

Behind the old gentleman young Mr Tipton-Martin produced a snort of quick disgust.

'That's very good of you,' said the old gentleman, handing over the wallet.

Mr Meiklejohn deftly extracted the card and gave it a glance.

'Mr Walter Grappelin,' he read. 'Thank you, sir.'

He was about to slip the card back into the old gentleman's wallet when he suddenly stopped and gave it another scrutiny.

'I'm verra sorry, sir,' he said, 'But this Ticket's out of date. It doesna' appear to have been renewed since …'

He stopped, and then continued in a voice from which he strove to eliminate the incredulity.

'… since 1943, sir.'

'Yes,' said old Mr Grappelin. 'Yes, that would be right. I suppose it must have been a year or so after that I last had occasion to use the Library. Just about the time of the end of the Second World War, the one with that chap Hitler, you know. I retired from my Editorship about then, and the Bodleian at Oxford has been sufficient for my needs up till now. But I found yesterday that I really ought to look up that novel of George Sand that was suppressed, you know, and the Bodleian hasn't a copy. So I thought I'd better come up here.'

'Quite so, sir,' said Mr Meiklejohn reassuringly. 'But I'm afraid you really will have to get your Ticket renewed. The office is just by the main entrance doors down there, sir. Round to your right.'

'Ah. Good. Thank you. Thank you.'

And the old man shuffled away, moving not much faster than the tortoise he so much resembled.

'Your Ticket, Mr Tipton-Martin, then,' Mr Meiklejohn said briskly.

'Oh. Er – er – ticket? Oh, yes, my Ticket.'

Young safari-suited Mr Tipton-Martin seemed not at all his usual whizzing self. Mrs Craggs wondered why.

And, for once, her curiosity was satisfied. Instead of shooting into the Reading Room and zipping round to secure himself some particularly advantageous desk, Mr Tipton-Martin stayed where he was and actually began to gossip with Mr Meiklejohn. To gossip. There was, thought Mrs Craggs, no other word for it.

'Do you know who that was?' he asked the warder.

'Gentleman name of Grappelin, sir.'

'Yes. But he's no ordinary gentleman. He's Professor Walter Grappelin. You know, the Editor of the *Oxford Dictionary of Nineteenth-Century French*, one of the great works of scholarship of our time. I thought he was dead years ago. The Dictionary came out in 1945, and he was quite old then. He retired as soon as he'd seen it through the press. He must be damned near a hundred now.'

'A verra remarkable man, sir,' said Mr Meiklejohn, in suitably awed tones. 'Verra remarkable indeed.'

Mr Tipton-Martin laughed. It was an unexpected sound. Mrs Craggs reckoned that whizzers didn't often laugh. But then this seemed to be a day of unexpected events.

'You may say old Walter Grappelin's remarkable,' Mr Tipton-Martin said. 'But he wasn't half as remarkable as his young brother.'

'Indeed not, sir? Then the younger Mr Grappelin must have been verra, verra remarkable.'

'He was. He was. He was the poet, you know.'

Mr Meiklejohn shook his head.

'I'm not verra much o' what you'd call a poetry man mesel', sir,' he said.

'No? I should have thought that everyone had heard of Maurice Grappelin. After all, next to Rupert Brooke he was probably our finest poet of the '14-'18 War.'

'Indeed, sir? Weel now, that's verra interesting.'

'That's as may be,' said Mr Tipton-Martin a little sharply. 'But the poetry's by no means the most interesting thing about Maurice Grappelin. Not many people remember this, or even know it. But he wasn't only a poet. He was a remarkable scholar as well. A philologist, of course, in the family tradition, following his elder brother's footsteps. But if you ask me, he'd have far outshone him if he'd lived. If his discoveries in the field of — But, never mind, you'd hardly understand.'

'The poor gentleman died early then, sir?' Mr Meiklejohn asked with undeterred sympathy.

'Died early?' Mr Tipton-Martin snapped. 'Why, he was killed, man. Killed in 1914. Didn't you even know that?'

'I'm afraid not, sir,' Mr Meiklejohn said.

He sounded thoroughly ashamed of his ignorance, and Mrs Craggs, who in the ordinary way would not have ventured to address a Reader, quite suddenly jumped into the conversation.

'An' 'ow come you know such a lot about his philol-whatsit an' all that?' she asked, politeness abandoned.

Mr Tipton-Martin looked affronted. As perhaps he had reason to be, suddenly spoken to by a person in a flowered apron with a rather squashed-looking red hat on her head.

'As a matter of fact,' he said, chilliness in every word, 'I work in the same discipline myself and I was also privileged, as an undergraduate, to re-catalogue the library at Castle Mandeville, a task which had been abandoned by none other than the young Maurice Grappelin at the outbreak of the 1914-18 War. So naturally I know something of the man, perhaps rather more than any other scholar in the field.'

And with that he turned on his heel and flounced into the Reading Room, omitting to show Mr Meiklejohn his Reader's Ticket.

But Mr Meiklejohn was unperturbed. He shook his head wonderingly.

'Losh,' he said, 'it's always amazing to me just how much a real scholar knows.'

Mrs Craggs sniffed.

'Real scholar,' she said.

'Och, come now, Mrs Craggs. The wee man's been spoken of as one of the rising people. There was a gentleman the other day who told me that when next month a certain learned journal comes out it's to have an article in it by the young man that's likely to astonish everybody in the field and make his name for him once and for all. Not that anyone else will ken what it's all about, mind. But in his wee world he's fair bent to be a king-pin.'

'That's as may be,' Mrs Craggs said, not at all impressed by this example of a whizzer whizzing. 'But all the same, he only

128

knew all about that Maurice Grappelin 'cos he happened to have had a job in the selfsame place where the feller worked afore he went off an' got shot for his country. I don't see what's so ruddy amazing about that.'

* * *

The next thing that happened on this day which was to turn out to be extraordinary in every way was that Mrs Milhorne lost her handbag. Mrs Milhorne had been a cleaner in the Reading Room for much the same time as Mrs Craggs had been. But her view of the Readers was not at all the same as her friend's. She regarded them all, scholars and whizzers alike, as creatures of an extraordinary, superior order, as not so much human beings with human beings' imperfections and weaknesses as walking Brains, beyond and above ordinary ways as the stars are above the humdrum earth.

So naturally when she realised she had left her handbag tucked into one of the knee-hole shelves at desk Number F8 when she had dusted it that morning she felt entirely incapable of simply going quietly into the Reading Room and retrieving it.

'I'd disturb them,' she said to Mrs Craggs, much as she might have been saying 'I'd assassinate them'. 'I couldn't do it. I couldn't. Me nerves would go all to pieces. I just could not set foot in That Room.'

'Then you'll have to manage without your old bag.'

'But I must have it. I must. It's got me pills in it. I need them pills. One every four hours I got to take. The Doctor said so.'

'Then go in and fetch it.'

'I couldn't. I can't. But I must have it. I must.'

Mrs Craggs sighed. She had known from the start what would happen in the end.

'All right,' she said. 'I'll go.'

And into the Reading Room with its ranks of bowed studious heads she went, walking quietly as she could but unable, of course, to do anything about her left shoe, which squeaked abominably and always had.

But only one intent reader took any notice, and that was a whizzer, one of the female variety, a lady dressed in a severe grey suit with a pointed nose and heavy purple-rimmed spectacles. She hissed at Mrs Craggs like an affronted goose. But otherwise nothing stopped her making her way between the radiating spokes of face-to-face desks with their high separating partitions until she got to Number F8.

She recognised at once its occupant. It was the old, old man, Professor Grappelin. He must have succeeded in renewing his Reader's Ticket without any trouble, she thought, and here he was now sitting patiently at this desk waiting for that book he wanted to come from where it must lie in the deep underground bookstores among the row on rows of close-packed volumes.

Or rather, Mrs Craggs thought, he ain't so much waiting as having a nice bit of a zizz till his book comes. He had, she saw, been reading a magazine, one of them magazines that the learned gents of the Reading Room were always reading. She could see its title. *The Journal of Philological Studies*. What ever 'philological' meant. And she could see the date on it, too. Today's date. The old boy still keeping up with all the latest, even if he was damn nearly a hundred years old.

She decided that she could probably rescue Mrs Milhorne's handbag from the knee-hole shelf without disturbing the old boy. And she would have succeeded in doing so, too. Only, just as she stooped to reach in beside the old chap's unmoving little frail body, a crumpled piece of paper that someone had dropped on the floor just under the desk caught her eye. Tidying-up was a discipline to Mrs Craggs. If there was dirt or mess about she could no more stop herself dealing with it than she could have stopped herself breathing. So she reached down and picked up the piece of paper – it was a sheet of plain paper, very stiff and just lightly squeezed together – and thrust it into the pocket in the front of her flowered apron with the intention of popping it into a wastepaper basket as soon as she had got out of the quietly calm atmosphere of the Reading Room.

But, in reaching just a little further so as to get hold of that piece of rubbish, the edge of her shoulder lightly brushed against the sleeping professor's jutting-out elbow. And when it did so the old, old man, his body weighing hardly more than that of any lucky little girl's giant doll, topped over out of his chair to lie, just in the position he had been in, curled up on the floor.

Mrs Craggs gasped. And then she gave a little short sharp involuntary scream.

Because, as the old man had fallen, his long grey muffler had come away and, looking down, Mrs Craggs's eyes had been drawn as if by two tugging black threads to the handle of a small shining silver paperknife that was protruding from the back of that frail old tortoise neck.

* * *

Mrs Craggs had recovered herself in a moment and had gone straight along to the central round desk to report the murder, all the more disturbed because of a nagging feeling at the back of her mind that somewhere before she had seen the murder weapon, that little silver paperknife. Its handle was funny. In the shape of a stubby, short-armed cross. She had seen that before somewhere, couldn't mistake it.

Just as she was about to report she noticed, a yard or two further round the counter, young Mr Tipton-Martin, standing waiting to hand back books he had finished with. So, remembering that he had known who old Professor Grappelin was, she went round, took him by the elbow and marched him back round, despite his initial protests, to help her tell her story.

It was a good thing she had done so, because, once a police constable had been summoned from the courtyard outside the Museum, Mr Tipton-Martin was able to advance matters in a decidedly swift way. Or so it seemed.

'Constable,' he said, when things had begun to be sorted out a little and they were waiting for the full might of Scotland Yard to arrive, 'there's something I think you ought to know.'

'Oh, yes, sir?'

'I hesitate to tell you, because it may seen like launching an accusation against a person who may be perfectly innocent. But on the other hand he is still here, and —'

'Who is this, sir?' the constable asked, with some urgency.

Mr Tipton-Martin pulled at the corners of the collar of his smart blue-and-white striped shirt.

'It's Francis Lecroix,' he said. 'I don't suppose you'll have ever heard of him, officer, but he's quite well known in his field, in a way. He's a philologist. Or he was. Well, he almost certainly still thinks of himself as one.'

'I'm sorry, sir,' said the constable. 'But I don't quite see what you're getting at.'

'No? No, I'm sorry. Well, you see, it's quite simple really. Lecroix years ago was one of Professor Grappelin's assistants on his great work, the *Oxford Dictionary of Nineteenth-Century French*. But he quarrelled with him. It was a professional disagreement over the definition of a certain group of words. And he resigned. And then, I'm afraid, he never got another job in the academic world. People thought he wasn't sound, you know. But he still persisted with his notion that Professor Grappelin had committed a serious crime in compiling that section of the Dictionary. He became obsessed with the idea. He even wrote a little book to explain his theories, and had it privately printed and copies sent to every philologist of note. It's very well known in its way, a sort of joke. Because, you see, the chap is mad, of course. Mad as a hatter. But he happens to be here in the Reading Room now, and it was today that Professor Grappelin suddenly surfaced when everybody thought he must be dead long ago.'

'I see, sir,' said the constable. 'And just where is this other gentleman now, this Mr – er – Lecroix, was it?'

'He's there, officer. Just there.'

And Mr Tipton-Martin extended a long arm and pointed right over to a far corner, just near Desk P9.

Mrs Craggs, who like everybody else had followed that long pointing arm, felt a sudden thump of dismay somewhere in the region of her heart. Because she recognised the man Mr Tipton-Martin had named. He was the old scholar she had once heard muttering to himself that 'a little learning is a dang'rous thing'. And, worse, the moment she saw him she knew where it was that she had seen that silver paperknife with the stubby cross handle. She had seen it more than once. On whatever desk it had been that Francis Lecroix was occupying. He always had it with him. He was always reading those old books that had uncut pages and he used the knife constantly to open them up.

Of course the constable had gone straight over and asked old Francis Lecroix – he must be seventy-five if he's a day, Mrs Craggs thought – to step over this way if he would. And there he had been by the Central Desk when from Scotland Yard to take charge of the inquiry there had arrived, with an impressive escort of detective-sergeants and fingerprint men and photographers and a scene-of-crime officer, the great towering form of Superintendent Mouse.

Mrs Craggs recognised him from his photo in the papers, that slab-sided six-foot-six-inches body, that solid wall of a face. But what she had never seen in the papers was what Superintendent Mouse pulled from the top pocket of his tent-like grey suit when Mr Tipton-Martin repeated his account of old Professor Grappelin, the *Oxford Dictionary of Nineteenth-Century French* and Mr Lecroix – a pair of heavy horn-rim spectacles. He put them on the bridge of his massive squabby nose and peered through them at little, safari-suited Mr Tipton-Martin.

'Hm,' he said. 'The *ODNCF*, eh? Masterly piece of work, of course. I do a little reading on those lines myself from time to time, and I couldn't do without it.'

Mr Tipton-Martin positively preened himself.

'Then perhaps you'll know that little book, *The Great Oxford Dictionary of Nineteenth-Century French Scandal*, Lecroix's polemic?' he said.

'Hm. Ha. Yes. Yes, interesting piece of work. In its way.'

'But the work of –' Mr Tipton-Martin dropped his voice since old Francis Lecroix was, after all, standing there blinking from one to the other – 'a total lunatic.'

'Oh, yes, yes. Undoubtedly. Lunatic, yes, lunatic.'

Superintendent Mouse removed his heavy hornrims and

tucked them decisively into his top pocket.

'Well, thank you, Mr – er – Tupton-Marlowe,' he said. 'And now I think, Mr Lecroix, if you'll accompany me to Scotland Yard we can have this business cleared up before very much longer.'

'Oh, no, you don't,' said Mrs Craggs.

She was surprised, really, to hear her own voice, right out loud like that in the tremendous hush that had fallen on the wide-domed Reading Room after the first excitement had died down. But she had spoken. The words had been forced out of her from somewhere.

And she was glad that they had.

But everyone was looking at her now. Superintendent Mouse's ham-like left hand was groping again for his hornrims. She had to justify what she had said.

'Look,' she began, 'you can't take him away like that. Well, there ain't no need to.'

Superintendent Mouse dropped the hornrims, which he had got half-way out of his top pocket, back in. Plainly this was not a matter where the more intellectual side of life could be called into play.

'You're the lady that found the body,' he pronounced. 'Cleaning woman, isn't it? Mrs Bloggs, I believe.'

'If you believe that, you'll believe anything that likes to come into your head,' Mrs Craggs retorted. 'No, name's Craggs, an' always has been ever since we was united more years ago than I cares to remember. An' if you believe a gentleman like old Mr Lecroix here, what's what I calls a real scholar, could've done what was done to that poor old professor, then you're worse nor what I thought.'

Superintendent Mouse drew himself up to his full six-foot-six. The breadth of his body was enormous.

'That's quite enough of that,' he said. 'When I want a charwoman to tell me who's a scholar and who isn't I'll sell every book in my library. I dare say Mr Lecroix here looks like a scholar to you, clothes he hasn't changed for the best part of six months and spectacles with their left lens cracked, but that

134

doesn't make him any different from any other person or persons. And he's got a little bit of explaining to do back at the Yard.'

He turned his massive bulk to face the aged author of *The Great Oxford Dictionary of Nineteenth-Century French Scandal*, who did indeed look a dusty and neglected figure.

'Now, just you come along with me,' he said.

But Mrs Craggs thrust herself, flowered apron, squashed red hat, between the Superintendent and his prey.

'He ain't going,' she said. How she brought herself to say it she never knew. 'He ain't going, or not until you've listened to reason for half a minute.'

'My good woman.'

'Don't you "good woman" me. An' just you listen. Mr Lecroix is a scholar. Ain't I seen him in here day after day? Nose down in those old books of his? Cutting away at every single page as has been stuck together ever since the book was printed and nobody else cared what was inside?'

But Superintendent Mouse's massive face had suddenly lit up with an inner fire.

'Cutting away at uncut pages?' he said. 'And what was he using to do that with? Come along now, speak up.'

It was then that Mrs Craggs thought that all she had done was to make matters worse for her nice old gentleman. But it was his knife that was still sticking deep into the frail neck of old Professor Grappelin, and she knew it was. And not telling the truth was not going to make matters one bit better for anyone.

So she told the truth. And Superintendent Mouse put on his heavy hornrims and went over and gave the shiny silver handle of the paperknife a short personal examination.

Then he returned to the Central Desk where the group of them were still standing.

'Yes,' he said. 'Well, come along now, Mr Lecroix.'

Mrs Craggs felt terrible. She knew that old Mr Lecroix, the man who could toddle out of the Reading Room muttering 'a little learning is a dang'rous thing', for all that he might have a bit of a bee in his bonnet about some complicated bit of studying in that huge big dictionary they were all on about, could not have plunged his paperknife into the old professor's neck and then covered up its jutting silver handle with the grey muffler. He could not have done that. It wasn't right for a man like him.

But how had his knife, his very own knife in the form of a cross, that she herself had seen him with so often, how could that knife have got to have been used for the horrible purpose that it had, if he was not the person who had used it?

And then she knew.

It came to her in a flash. No, old Mr Lecroix, the real scholar, had not used that knife. It had been used by none other than Mr Tipton-Martin, whizzer. She realised that not only did she know this, but she knew why Mr Tipton-Martin had done what he had done.

No wonder he had gabbled and gabbled on like that after the sudden appearance of the old, old professor when everyone had thought he was long ago dead. Professor Walter Grappelin, whose brother had been Maurice Grappelin, the poet who had been tragically killed in 1914. The poet and the philol-whatsit. A philol-whatsit like Mr Tipton-Martin himself, Mr Tipton-Martin who had once worked in a library somewhere where Maurice Grappelin had been working until he had dropped everything to go and fight in the war. Had left behind – she knew this to be true, as if she had seen the evidence with her own eyes – some discovery or other in philol-whatsit that young Tipton-Martin years later had found. Had found and had pinched, safe in the knowledge that no one would know that Maurice Grappelin had done the work before him. Only, what was more likely than that Walter Grappelin would recognise his brilliant young brother's work when, just next month, it came out in the *Journal of Philolthingamebob Studies*? The very magazine the old, old man had been reading this month's copy of just before he had fallen asleep at his desk over there.

And young whizzer Tipton-Martin had realised his danger, and then had realised that the perfect scapegoat for the murder that would get him out of his trouble and let him whizz on up to being king-pin of philol-whatsit was there in the Reading Room, asking to be made use of. Even down to providing him with a weapon that would point back to its owner like a ruddy illuminated street-sign.

But how was she to prove all this? How was she to convince Superintendent Mouse when plainly he had lapped up every word that his fellow so-called scholar, young Safari Suit, had ladled out to him?

Old Mr Lecroix had said hardly a word up till now. He had agreed that he was who he was, but beyond that he had kept silent, looking from face to face as each development occurred. But now he spoke.

'Grappelin was wilfully mistaken over the vocabulary of the *midinettes*,' he said. 'Wilfully, you know. You've only to read my book to see why. But I wouldn't have wished him any harm.'

'There,' said Mrs Craggs. 'There. You see. Mild as Dutch cheese. 'Ow can you say he'd of done a thing like that?'

'Mrs Bloggs,' said Superintendent Mouse, 'I should be reluctant to have you charged with obstruction, but, believe me, I shall if you persist in this.'

His huge left hand reached up to his hornrims as if he would like just to peruse the relevant section of the Act before instituting proceedings.

It's now or never, thought Mrs Craggs. Whatever shall I do?

And then – then, as if the spirit of Athene, goddess of wisdom, had descended on her from the great domed roof above, the answer came to her. She had had it. She had had it all along.

So now she produced it. It came out of her pocket, out of the pocket of her flowered apron. A piece of crumpled paper. A stiff lightly crumpled sheet of paper.

'Look,' she said. 'Just you look at this, an' you'll see.'

So charged were her words that Superintendent Mouse, manoeuvring his huge bulk round in the direction of the Readers' Entrance and extending a ham fist in the direction of old Mr Lecroix's elbow, stopped and swung himself back round again.

'Look at what?' he demanded.

'Look at this piece o' paper what I picked up just under old Professor Grappelin's desk,' Mrs Craggs said. 'Get your old hornrims out, mate, and have a gander at this. Look, a piece of paper, stiff paper what's been wrapped round something. Ain't it? Ain't it?'

Superintendent Mouse, who, to do him justice, had ignored the word 'mate' and had got out his hornrims and settled them across the bridge of his great squabby nose, peered and agreed.

'Yes. Stiff paper and wrapped round an object.'

'An' you know why, don't you?' said Mrs Craggs. 'Fingerprints. That's why. Well, if someone was keen to keep his fingerprints off of that there paperknife, it can only have been 'cos it wasn't the chap who owned the knife what used it. Everyone knew it was old Mr Lecroix's knife, so there wouldn't have been no point in him keeping his paw marks off it, would there? An', look, you can see the print o' that there cross handle on the paper, can't you? Can't you?'

Mr Tipton-Martin began to sidle very gently in the direction of the Readers' Entrance. But Superintendent Mouse, moving his great bulk with surprising speed, put it between him and the wide open spaces beyond. Then he looked at Mrs Craggs.

'It's Mrs – Mrs Craggs, isn't it?' he said. 'Well, just give your full name and address to one of my officers, Mrs Craggs. I have a feeling we'll be needing you to give evidence sooner or later, and a witness who really knows what she's talking about is always a pleasure to have on hand.'

And from old Mr Lecroix there came a murmured rider to that statement.

'Yes,' he said, almost as if he was speaking to himself, 'drink deep or taste not the Pierian spring.'

That's been very helpful. But can you give me some more facts, facts about Mrs Craggs's actual life?

Facts about her life? Well I don't think nobody knows more about that than what I do. Unless it's her Creator. Let me see. Well, I said she was country-born, didn't I? An' – well, it's funny how you don't know so much about a person until somethink they does, or somethink they has to do, sort of brings out things about them. I mean, like the way she likes reading them crime books from time to time, like when I persuaded her to go to romantic Spain. Bit different from what we usually does together, but then somehow that was like as if someone 'ad – had wanted us to be a sort of story in some newspaper when they 'ad – had a Summer Number. That was when I found out she liked those Agatha Christie things, though I don't believe she reely guessed who done – whom it was what did it before that Porrot did. I mean, it's *Dame* Agatha, so it stands to reason she'd know best, doesn't it? You know, I sometimes think Mrs Craggs's life's more like a lot o' them fairy stories, reely I do.

IX

MRS CRAGGS AND THE PALE ELLA

'Evil under the sun,' said Mrs Milhorne. 'I wouldn't care for that.'

Mrs Craggs sniffed loudly and lowered her Agatha Christie to the sand beside her chair.

It was the ninth time she had to do so that morning, and now she was within a few pages of the denouement.

'Nah, I dare say as you wouldn't much care for a spot of evil,' she said. 'Not with your nerves, what you've mentioned before.'

Mrs Milhorne, in bright, wildly over-young two-piece swimsuit, spread full-length on a sun-lounger and, still untanned, looking to her friend's eyes something like a stretch of suet-pudding held together with a couple of coloured handkerchiefs, responded to this tribute to her sensitivity with a deep sigh, acquiescent and suffering.

'But there ain't no real evil in the story neither,' Mrs Craggs felt bound to add.

'Don't you like it then?'

''Course I like it. Wouldn't have gorn on with it if I didn't. Wouldn't have almost finished it.'

Mrs Milhorne made a token effort to raise her head and look down towards the book.

141

'You haven't finished?' she said. 'I quite thought you had. I'm sure I'd of never interrupted otherwise.'

'No, I'm sure you wouldn't,' Mrs Craggs said. 'But it don't matter. I knows who done it now. It'll all turn out to be a plot between the husband an' his wife, the one what's supposed to be so mousey but every now an' again forgets. You see, she lay on a beach pretending to be the victim, so that he had a' alibi an' could do the killing later. The victim was an actress, name o' Arlena. Arlena Stuart. An' it looks like a love triangle, but it ain't. Silly really, but a bit o' make-believe ain't so bad when you're on holiday.'

'Well, of course, I can't follow all that, except the love triangle,' Mrs Milhorne said, getting up on one skinny elbow. 'But I don't see as 'ow that's silly. That's real life, if you ask me. Passion.'

'Real life's dirt,' said Mrs Craggs. 'As well you ought to know.'

'Oh, no. No. It's … Well, real real-life's like what it is round here. Gypsies and bull-fighters, fiestas and that flamingo dancing, them lacy mantillas and fluttering fans. That's life. Life lived to the full.'

'You been reading the brochure.'

'No, I haven't,' said Mrs Milhorne (who had). 'And I'll tell you what: it's happening right here in front of our eyes, a love triangle. I seen it.'

'Pooh, old Reg Chilworth over there an' his Vera with that Frank Stewart?'

'You noticed too?'

'Course I have. But that little old to-do ain't much cop in the evil stakes. A set-in-his-ways stockroom clerk going on fifty an' his wife what's two or three years younger an' wants a last fling.'

Mrs Milhorne pouted. 'Well,' she said, 'Frank's a real Dong Juan, that you can't deny. Rolling in money, too, and determined to have what he wants, cost what it may. And, listen, his name: it's just the same as in your book. Stewart.'

Mrs Craggs looked down the beach to where the three

subjects of their conversation sat on the hot sand, little dumpy Reg Chilworth a significant three yards distant from the other two.

'Oh, yes,' she said. 'Won't tell none o' the rest of the package how he makes all that money he seems to have, an' out here all on his ownio. Frank Stewart, man o' mystery, getting a bit heavy round the tum. Cor.'

'You wait,' said Mrs Milhorne darkly. 'You wait. Something'll happen there before our fortnight's up. You mark my words.'

Mrs Craggs retrieved *Evil Under the Sun* and dealt with its last pages. She had been quite right: the husband and wife had actually been in collusion and the murder not the outcome of a love triangle but of good old-fashioned greed.

* * *

'We could have a go in one of them what they calls pedalos,' Mrs Milhorne said next day, restless on her sun-lounger but demonstrative with such tourist Spanish as she had acquired.

Mrs Craggs laid down *The Murder of Roger Ackroyd*.

'I may be on holiday,' she said. 'But I ain't going back to me blessed childhood.'

Mrs Milhorne bridled.

'And you with your head buried in those whodunits,' she said. 'That's childish enough, if you ask me.'

'Maybe. But it ain't so stupid as getting yourself in a muck sweat bobbing about on the briny in a blinking pedal-boat. Look at Vera Chilworth an' her man o' mystery out there.'

And, true enough, the two of them were sending their little boat round and round in aimless circles in the sea, squealing with laughter all the while. And sitting with pink, sunburnt flesh close pressed against pink, sunburnt flesh.

'It's more like they're making a fool of Reg Chilworth,' Mrs Milhorne commented bodefully. 'Look at him, there on the sand. There's someone taking life serious. Deadly serious.'

'You think so? Well, I think working out who killed Roger

143

Ackroyd's every bit as serious as him.'

'Oh, no. You can't think that. I mean, a book. Who cares who killed Roger Ackroyd?'

'I do,' said Mrs Craggs. 'An' if you'd just shut up, I'll make out who did.'

Mrs Milhorne's affronted silence lasted just four and a half minutes.

'All the same,' she said abruptly, 'you can't really blame her. Taking the fearful risk. Not when Reg behaves the way he does. Fret and fume over everything like a little Hitler.'

'But them shrimps in that Pale Ella stuff *was* off,' Mrs Craggs answered, once more consigning Roger Ackroyd to the sand. 'I smelt 'em.'

'How do you know I was talking about the paella?' Mrs Milhorne demanded, as if somehow her privacy had been invaded.

'First off,' Mrs Craggs explained wearily, 'you was looking at old Reg. An' then after a bit you screwed your face up like as if something was repeating on you. Easy.'

'Well, all right, now you've said it. But that doesn't alter the way Reg went on. Picking the shrimps out one by one and putting them in his wine glass to show to the Representative. I ask you.'

Mrs Craggs chuckled.

'He'll have a pretty long wait with his old shrimps if he hangs on to 'em till that Rep comes round to our hotel again,' she said. 'Assistance an' information throughout your holiday, that's a laugh.'

'I thought he was very nice that first day,' Mrs Milhorne replied, with a toss of her lank curls.

Mrs Craggs gave a deep laugh.

'That was 'cos you hoped to get off with him,' she said.

'I never.'

'You did. Bad as old Frank Stewart, desperate for a touch o' romance before it's past all hope.'

'I am going to go into the sea,' said Mrs Milhorne. She rose from her sun-lounger in a series of angular jerks. 'And as for

Frank Stewart,' she added, 'you can't argue but that he's soyg-nee. He's never one to complain about the food. *Tomates rellenos, por favor, waiter*, that's him every time.'

And off she marched.

'Don't you get run down by one o' them pee-day-lows,' Mrs Craggs called after her. 'We don't want no mystery deaths on this here holiday.'

* * *

The day after that was even hotter, and Mrs Milhorne had to move up out of the sun to the hotel patio in order to interrupt her friend's reading of *Murder at the Vicarage* (Mrs Craggs had cared enough about who had killed Roger Ackroyd to have had her suspicions confirmed before the late Spanish dinner the night before).

'That Miss Flynn,' Mrs Milhorne said after a silence of some seven minutes. 'There's her too.'

Mrs Craggs lowered Miss Marple to the marble-chip floor.

'Yeh,' she said. 'She makes a nice fourth at that table o' theirs in the dining-room, fourth side for your precious old triangle.'

'That's all very well,' Mrs Milhorne replied. 'But what you can't deny is that that creature definitely made a play for Frank Stewart in the plane. And he wouldn't have none of her. A woman scorned. I'll say no more.'

''Ere,' said Mrs Craggs, who had not taken those last four words quite at their face value, 'wouldn't you like to borrow one o' me Christies. *Evil Under the Sun*, that'd keep your head down.'

'I told you. I couldn't never follow all that trickery. And, besides, Life's providing me with a real drama.'

'Oh, yus. Little Reg Chilworth straight from counting his bits an' pieces in the stockroom and the mysterious and dashing Frank Stewart chucking his money an' his Tomaters Real Enos around. I know.'

'There's an atmosphere,' Mrs Milhorne countered, unde-terred. 'I can feel it, even if others can't.'

'Atmosphere? That's them shrimps from the Pale Ella still ponging out the back.'

And Mrs Craggs resolutely returned to trace out step by step, word for word, the shocks awaiting the Vicar of St Mary Mead.

Mrs Milhorne remained silent for less than half a minute. Her friend's attitude had rankled.

'What about that Gunther Gross chap, then?' she demanded abruptly. 'Don't tell me he isn't sinister, the way he keeps asking our party if anyone wants to go across to Tangiers, instead of sticking to the German package where he belongs.'

Mrs Craggs did no more than grunt at this.

'And I saw him with Vera Chilworth yesterday,' Mrs Milhorne went on. 'Alone. Teet-a-teet. I say no more.'

But Mrs Craggs was comparing impersonation as hinted at in Miss Marple's current inquiry with the trick as it had been used in M. Poirot's encounter under the sun.

Yet after a little, when she thought she had begun to see what the answer was going to be, she raised her head.

''Spect our Vera weren't finding her Frank quite the sweeper-off-of-her-feet she'd counted on,' she said. 'I think he works in a bank.'

'Never,' said Mrs Milhorne hotly. 'A man with red blood in his veins work in a bank? Ministry of Defence, *I* think, which is why he can't tell us where all that money comes from.'

Mrs Craggs headed back towards St Mary Mead.

'That's as may be,' she said in farewell. 'But he had a pretty smart way o' counting up his pee-see-tars when I saw him change one of his travellers cheques yesterday.'

'We'll see,' countered Mrs Milhorne. 'We'll see. And don't blame me if Tragedy ensues.'

* * *

And it was that very evening that tragedy, or something at least, did ensue. Most of the package were assembled in the hotel bar waiting with edgy impatience for that late, late Spanish dinner.

Reg and Vera Chilworth were at a corner table accompanied

as ever by Frank Stewart, wearing even indoors a coloured sombrero he had bought at the airport. Looking at it, Mrs Craggs recorded how loose it appeared on a neat haircut that spoke to her more of the teller's window than the secret agent's observation eyrie.

Alone at a distance from the noisy laughter rising up from Vera and Frank, Miss Flynn, no doubt contemplating the out-of-it fourth she was soon to make at their dinner table, slowly sipped a bitter lemon.

Suddenly squat little well-beamed Reg Chilworth jumped up and went out. Mrs Craggs watched him idly as he waddled determinedly across to the hotel's pair of erratic lifts.

'Come on, Frank,' Vera Chilworth promptly called in a voice so loud that no one in the whole bar could have failed to hear. 'Plenty of time for another one for us before dinner.'

Mrs Milhorne peered at the tiny diamanté evening watch that was her great pride.

'I don't know,' she said, 'I could have sworn it was all but time to eat.'

'Tummy rumbling, dear?' Mrs Craggs asked.

'Well, I'm sure my watch isn't wrong,' Mrs Milhorne went on, ignoring the crudity and giving the little glittering object a good shake. 'But then sometimes it does lose. Or gain.'

'If it ain't stopped altogether,' Mrs Craggs said uncompromisingly.

But at that moment the plump Germanic form of Herr Gunther Gross from the other party loomed up, and there followed a complicated exchange involving 'ten minutes for nine' and 'ten minutes to, we say, or do I mean past?' To this Mrs Craggs contributed nothing. Instead she sat in silent thought.

Her cogitation was interrupted dramatically. Mrs Milhorne gave a little screech.

'There,' she said, 'that proves it. There's Reg Chilworth slipping into the dining-room, and he goes in on the dot of nine every night. On the dot.'

'Nah,' said Mrs Craggs, 'there's a full ten minutes yet. I can trust me own stomach, even if no one else can't.'

Yet all the same after a few moments she got to her feet and made for the dining-room's broad double-doors. Mrs Milhorne trailed along in bewildered pursuit.

'I don't understand,' she wailed. 'Where are you going? If it isn't time ...'

But there was no sign of Reg Chilworth in the wide expanse of the dining-room when Mrs Craggs thrust open the main doors. At each little table four places were set with shrimp-stuffed *tomates rellenos* awaiting each guest. For a second Mrs Craggs stood and thought. Then she marched over to the table which she and her friend shared with a permanently interclasped honeymoon couple. From it she picked up the tomato-half from her own place and tramped across with it to the window table normally occupied by the Chilworths, Frank Stewart and Miss Flynn.

'What ever are you doing?' whined Mrs Milhorne.

Mrs Craggs did not answer. She stood picturing in her mind where exactly each of the table's occupants would sit. And then she pounced.

She seized the shrimp-crammed hors d'oeuvre awaiting the debonair, if podgy, Frank Stewart and replaced it swiftly with her own, and then, turning to the open window nearby, with a single vigorous jerk she sent the tomato-half flying far down on to the beach below.

'What – what 'ave you done?' bleated Mrs Milhorne.

Mrs Craggs gave a short sigh.

'Well, I'm not a hundred per cent sure,' she said, 'but I think it's a good idea to have got rid o' that Tomater Real Enos. O' course, old Reg putting those bad shrimps what he's been keeping into it would probably only give our Dong Juan a nasty dose o' the bellyaches. But best be on the safe side.'

A look of slow-dawning understanding spread over Mrs Milhorne's countenance.

'You mean ... You mean ...' she said.

'I mean that's about the size o' your dramatic murder,' Mrs Craggs answered. 'It ain't no woman scorned, and it ain't no

148

wicked foreigner smuggling drugs what's only another lonely-heart wanting to air his English. An' it certainly ain't no murder for money made to look like a love triangle. But it is real life all right, if that's what you wants.'

Yes. But, I wonder, can you go really far back into her life? A childhood friend would be ideal.

Well, I know she's supposed to have been born in the country an' to be ever so down to earth because of it. But what I say is head in the air's nicer than down in all that mud and stuff any day. And sometimes I wonder. Well, some of them plants she mentions, an' makes use of, if we're to believe half what she says, well, I don't believe they exist reely. I mean, Devil's Snitchbane an' Vomit Weed, reely nasty. An' she keeps on about that last one being in the Chelsea Physic Garden, too. Well, that's a proper scientific place, even if it is hundreds of years old, an' I don't think they'd have somethink there that might be somethink a story-writer made up just because it'd fit in nicely with the tale he wanted to tell. That's lying, that is, an' I don't think it's at all nice. Not what I call nice, anyhow.

X

Mrs Craggs Gives a Dose of Physic

ONE OF THE PLACES IN London to which Mrs Craggs once brought her vigorous elbows was the Chelsea Physic Garden. She worked for the wife of the new curator there, scrubbing and polishing away at the house which stands at the top of that unlikely four acres of well-cultivated ground running down to the Thames, hardly more than two miles from the very centre of the capital.

She liked the job, even though she did not get on well with Mrs Bount, the curator's wife. Mrs Bount hated the old house that was newly hers, and Mrs Craggs liked the house, a solid Victorian place, and even more the Garden beyond it.

'Oh, Mrs Craggs, do stop rubbing and rubbing away at those perfectly awful tiles. If we do have to stay here, they're going to be replaced by some decent stainless steel, I promise you that.'

Mrs Craggs's elbow continued to shunt determinedly to and fro.

'Can't see what you got against 'em,' she said. 'They been 'ere ever since the house has. Got a right to stay, if you ask me. Besides, all these little pictures 'o flowers on 'em. That's just right for the Garden.'

'And what about all those little cracks and chips on them?

153

Are they just right too? Swarming with microbes and bacteria. You take my word for it. It's a wonder the children are still alive after a year with this kitchen.'

It's a wonder they're still a couple of healthy little devils, Mrs Craggs said to herself, after the way you-go worrying on at them with your medicines to stop this and your medicines to stop that.

The curator's wife was a fervid believer in taking advantage of every latest scientific discovery, and she was quick to keep Mrs Craggs informed about each newest revelation.

But Mrs Craggs was careful to shut her more disparaging thoughts well inside her head. She had no intention of losing her job. She liked the whole place too much to risk that. She liked the singing of the birds, so loud and constant that it overrode – well, sort of – the thrumming of the traffic along the wide road of the Embankment at the far end of the Garden. She liked every one of the plants and trees growing peacefully away behind the high, sheltering red-brick walls. She liked the old statue of Sir Hans Sloane that presided over the Garden, old Sir Hans who in days long past had leased the ground in perpetuity to the Worshipful Society of Apothecaries to grow herbs and medicinal plants in, and who stood there now, his bewigged head green-faced from some quietly growing lichen and white-crowned from bird droppings. She liked the words carved in the soft white stone of the statue's base. About it being put up so that the founders' 'Successors and Posterity may never forget their Common Benefactor'.

She was not quite sure whether she herself counted as a Successor or a Posterity. But she often gave the old boy a little nod and murmured, 'Shan't forget, mate', as she passed by.

When her morning's work in the house was over she never failed, rain or shine, to take a little toddle along the Garden's intersecting paths. She had been a bit shy of doing so in her first days there because the Garden, which is first of all still a research establishment, was not open to the public. Only on two or three days in the year were people who had no special reason for being allowed inside admitted.

But soon Mrs Craggs discovered that there were always

liable to be one or two botany students wandering about. And before long she felt she had taken her proper place beside a certain white-bearded old gentleman with very pink skin and a pair of pince-nez, or the lady who, winter and summer, was always dressed in an enveloping dull-grey macintosh surmounted by a matching dull-grey round hat – once Mrs Craggs saw her carefully replacing half a dozen seedlings of a particularly prolific plant which one of the gardeners had just hoed out – or the various gaunt-faced, bachelor-looking men in wire-rimmed spectacles, mostly askew, meticulously filling notebook after notebook with observations.

None of the gardeners, who were not the ancient fellows in smocks who might have been expected but mostly young men and girls who favoured, sensibly, blue jeans as they stooped and knelt at the beds, ever asked her what she was doing as she walked up and down the neat grass or gravel paths. So, with the best of them, she peered away at all the different growing things. And she loved them all. She loved even the Order Beds where plants were arranged in a solemn procession of botanical families from the Ranunculaceae to the Gramineae. 'Grasses, I call 'em,' she would murmur when her daily walk happened to take her to that culminating point in the grand sequence.

She loved the exotics and she loved the home-spun. She rejoiced in plants she had been told had been brought from distant lands to the Garden as much as three hundred years before. There was the pink periwinkle from Madagascar. There was the starry yellow Forsythia, named after William Forsyth who had had charge of the Garden in the year 1770. And especially there was the wide-spreading Chinese willow-pattern tree near the old Students Gate, locked firmly nowadays with a big brass padlock and provided with a little, never-used bell in a little protective cage.

But she loved equally the flowers and shrubs known to her as a girl in the unspoilt countryside of her distant youth, and the hardy survivors such as she had grown herself in the brick and tarmac London of her early married life. There was, beneath a pretty little curly-trunked foreign tree labelled *Salix matsudana tortuosa*, a clump of London Pride. Its old lead name-plate called it '*Saxifraga geum*. var. *dentata*'. But Mrs Craggs knew better. There was, too, at the right time of year, a splendidly healthy clump of *Lobelia inflata* in the Campanulaceae section of the Order Beds, quite as good as some she had once in a pot on the window-sill of her first married home. She remembered this same plant from her childhood as well, when it had grown wild under the prosaic name of vomit weed. It had been a ritual in those far-off times to terrorise any playmate who had transgressed against their private laws into chewing enough of the leaves and tiny pods to produce a satisfactory retributive sicking-up. Mrs Craggs gave a reminiscent chuckle whenever she saw those little bright-blue flowers on their tiny-leaved stalks.

Yet for all her delight in the peace and placidity of the Garden the day was to come when shrieks and yells disturbed its calm, and sudden death seemed to intrude on this oasis dedicated to renewing and preserving the principle of life.

* * *

It happened one sunny June morning. Mr Bount had finished lecturing to a group of students from London University. It was his custom at this time to take a cup of tea. Only, instead of tea from India, he liked to drink a decoction made from one or other of the herbs in the Garden itself. It might be mint tea. It might be strawberry-leaf tea. It might even be dandelion tea, brewed from a handful of leaves of one of the weeds which shared the well-cultivated ground with plants that had perhaps more right to be there.

Weeds, in fact, were one of the minor sources of contention that sent occasional ripples across what ought to have been the ever-calm surface of life inside the Garden's high brick walls. The trouble sprang from Mr Bount's predecessor, an aged, aged gentleman who had held his office for something like sixty years. Towards the end he had allowed weeds to flourish almost unchecked. He had been known, indeed, to rebuke a gardener at work 'dressing the beds' – this eighteenth-century term for planting-out is still used – for pulling up even one weed. 'Anything that grows, grows not because of us but because of the power that is in it,' he would say. 'We're glad that the kowhai plant that came from Captain Cook's New Zealand expedition has seeded itself time and again here. We should be just as glad to see daisies and dandelions springing up from their own seeds.'

Indeed, Mr Bount had actually secured his curatorship over this very question of weeds. There had been only one other serious contender, a Dr Crippen, a man really a good deal better qualified in the way of degrees and fellowships, a real scientific out-and-outer. He had put before the interview board a sweeping plan to transform the Garden into 'an absolutely efficient research instrument', pledging that within a year of his taking office not a plant would grow that was not in its proper place and for a proper purpose. The board, at first almost overwhelmed, had at last quailed at the thought of this onslaught. They had asked Mr Bount – no doctor he – for his views. 'Well,' he had answered, 'I don't see the harm in a weed or two here and there. I'd rather the gardeners encouraged plants that need care than spent time grubbing up harmless little fellows. I mean, whether it grows in the medicinal plants area or pops up where it will, I've quite a fondness for *Taraxacum officinale*.' And so haphazard dandelions were saved and Mr Bount rather than Dr Crippen became Curator.

But weeds continued to be a source of conflict. Dr Crippen was not a man to retire from the field, however much he recognised that final victory was not to be his. He might not be Curator of the Chelsea Physic Garden but he was a recognised student of botany, indeed a distinguished practitioner in the science. So he had a right to visit the Garden with frequency. And when he did so he seldom failed to have a word with easy-going Mr Bount about the number of weeds to be seen between the rows in the living reference book of the Order Beds, or in cracks in the ancient stones of the steps leading down from the nobly padlocked Students Gate or in the paths between the various greenhouses, or anywhere and everywhere.

So on that sunny June morning he launched yet another attack in the half-hour when poor Mr Bount was quietly sipping his dandelion tea, sitting out in a canvas chair on the paving-stones in front of the creeper-hung laboratory building next to his house.

'I see you've got a lot of *Senecio aureus* down by the Embankment Gates, Bount,' he said, marching up and firing his shot without preliminary.

Mr Bount took a sip of his hot tea.

'Well, yes,' he said, 'I've been keeping an eye on that. Very vigorous growth, very vigorous.'

'I dare say it is. But it shouldn't be there, you know. It's a weed. The Garden doesn't exist to foster nuisances.'

'Oh, I know. It ought to be seen to perhaps. But that area in front of the Gates is a dead loss, you know. I mean, we haven't used the gates for years, but they were given to the Garden by generous benefactors so I don't see that we can really open up a bed or two in front of them, and the ragwort might as well live out its day there as not. It's a cheerful little fellow. Always reminds me of the sun, you know, in sort of miniature.'

'Does it?' snapped Dr Crippen. 'Well, all it reminds me of is that you're ruining a great botanical garden.'

Mr Bount took another sip of his dandelion tea.

'Well, I wouldn't exactly say "ruining",' he answered. 'Keeping going. That's rather more the idea I have of my work here. And, really, I intend to go on doing it just as I am.'

It was a mildly expressed retort. But it seemed to drive Dr Crippen to a new pitch of anger. He stood looking down on his seated rival, and his thin-cheeked face, normally as pale as the flowers of *Lilium candidum*, the Madonna lily, swiftly went as scarlet as the hectic blooms of *Kniphofia* var. *Mount Etna*, the red-hot poker. Then he turned and marched away down the wide gravelled path leading to the statue of Sir Hans Sloane and on to the Embankment Gates, there to disappear from view among the lusty early summer growths.

Mr Bount drained his cup.

'My dear,' he called out to his wife through the open windows of their house, 'could you possibly make me another cup? That was delicious.'

In her kitchen Mrs Bount shot the furious glance she would have liked to direct at her huband full on to innocent old Mrs Craggs.

'Why can't he have tea from a tea-bag and save all that awful mess?' she demanded. 'The tea-bag is one of the few decent technological advances made in kitchen-work. But will he take advantage of it? Never.'

'Well, I don't go much by them bags meself,' Mrs Craggs answered soothingly 'You can't never tell what's in 'em. That's what I say.'

'They are made by machines in properly hygienic conditions,' Mrs Bount replied. 'You can't do better than that.'

Mrs Craggs, by way of unspoken rebuke to that crushing remark, went across and filled Mrs Bount's new rapid-boil kettle with water for the dandelion brew, a wifely duty Mrs Bount had neglected in her zeal for extolling modernity.

'Not but what,' Mrs Craggs added, as she switched the kettle on, 'that old hubby 'o yours won't have gone an' started to look at his blessed plants before this is half-way ready.'

She gave a cackle of a laugh. Mr Bount's enthusiasm for everything that grew in the Garden, even for *Taraxacum officinale* and *Senecio aureus*, those interlopers, was a source of pleasure to her. And it stayed so, however often it meant that she had to go plunging about the greenhouses and Order Beds looking for him when the telephone rang or there was a caller.

And, sure enough, after the second cup of dandelion tea had been made and she had taken it outside, Mr Bount's chair was empty.

'Tea up,' she called loudly, loudly enough to add a good discordant sound to the song of the birds and the thrum of traffic in the soft air of the Garden.

She got no response.

159

'Oh, well,' she announced, 'I'm leaving it. If it's cold when you come for it, whose fault is that?'

She tramped back indoors and began giving the Curator's drawing-room a dusting drastic enough to take the very paint off the window ledges.

Before long, however, it was brought to her notice that the Curator had come back to his chair and had swallowed his cup of cooling dandelion tea. Brought to her notice in a horribly startling way.

* * *

Coming in through the open windows she heard a terrible rasping sound. At first she thought it was issuing from downstairs and was Mrs Bount's new-model vacuum-cleaner gone more than a little wrong. She had been expecting the machine, which had a fearsome number of gadgets attached to it, to blow up ever since Mrs Bount had first proudly shown it to her. But in a moment she realised that Mrs Bount never touched the thing herself and that the sound was coming in from outside and was, as well, one that could not have been made by any machine. It was a human sound. But an appalling one.

Quickly she went over to a window and looked out.

There on the sunlit old paving-stones in front of the laboratory she saw Mr Bount. He was stretched rigid in his canvas chair, eyes wide open and staring. And from his mouth there was coming that fearful sound. It was his breathing, his grinding attempts to draw breath.

Mrs Craggs rushed out, calling loudly for Mrs Bount.

It was plain to both of them when they got to the Curator that somehow he had become very dangerously ill. When he saw the two women, he managed to force out a few words, though they were hardly comprehensible.

'Light, light,' he seemed to be repeating. 'Light. Hurts. Light.'

He made efforts to put a forearm over his eyes as if to ward off the clear June sunlight that only half an hour earlier he had made a point of seeking.

'He's been poisoned.'

The voice came from behind them as they bent anxiously over the stricken man. They both whirled round. It was Dr Crippen.

'What you mean, poisoned?' Mrs Craggs demanded, her mind at once filled with the notion that because the defeated rival for the Garden curatorship had the same name as the notorious murderer of old he must somehow be responsible for the horrible thing that was happening to Mr Bount.

'It's obvious, woman,' Dr Crippen snapped. 'Look at that cup there on the ground. Dandelion tea, wasn't it? Nothing easier than to add a noxious substance to that. Belladonna is my diagnosis, all the classic symptoms. And there's a fine specimen of *Solanum belladonna* in the Garden, right to hand.'

'Belladonna,' Mrs Craggs echoed. 'That's deadly nightshade, ain't it? That's a killer. A killer.'

'You're perfectly correct,' Dr Crippen said coldly. 'And, if I'm right, and I have no doubt that I am, Bount needs help urgently. You shouldn't be standing there wailing.'

Mrs Craggs found time, just time, to feel a dart of anger. She had not been wailing, even if Mrs Bount certainly was making an odd noise somewhere between little screams and a whimper. And, what's more, they had only just arrived on the scene. But she suppressed the feeling at once. This was an emergency. There were things to be got on with.

'The doctor,' she said. 'I'll ring the doctor. His name's just on top of the phone, nice an' clear on account of the kiddies. I'll go.'

'Yes, yes,' Mrs Bount managed to say. 'The doctor. Get him. Get him quickly, Mrs Craggs.'

Mrs Craggs headed for the house.

'No,' snapped Dr Crippen, in a voice of strong authority.

Mrs Craggs stopped for an instant and turned her head.

'Not a simple family doctor, for heaven's sake. This is a specialised matter. Ring St Margaret's Hospital. There's a

161

Poisons Unit there, I happen to know.'

Mrs Craggs was not sure that it would not still be best to get the Bount family doctor. He lived quite near, she remembered. But Dr Crippen – pity he was only a sort of scientist and not a proper doctor – did seem to know what he was talking about.

She hurried on inside, found the telephone directories, selected the correct volume, took it over to where the fresh sunlight poured in at a window so that she could read the small print and, giving her thumb a substantial lick, rapidly turned the pages in search of the hospital number.

She found it after a little bother. What did they want to go and put 'St' for 'Saint' under the Sa- names for? She dialled. In good trenchant terms she told whoever answered what had happened. She received a promise that 'The Team' would be round almost immediately.

'They'd better come in by what we calls the West Gate,' she said. 'It's in Royal Hospital Road, just to the side of the house. Only, no one might hear you ringing at the house door, an' the West Gate's always open in the day. There's a notice saying 'Authorised Visitors Only', but you don't want to take no notice o' that.'

She waited until she was sure she had been understood and then rang off. She paused for a moment, took a deep breath and dialled the police.

'I think you'd better come round,' she said when she had got on to someone who sounded important. 'There's been murder done 'ere, or I'm a Dutchman.'

Back outside, she found that moment by moment it was looking as if it was murder, rather than attempted murder, that had been done. Mr Bount was even worse. His breathing was still more strained and his limbs were twitching and jerking. The light seemed to be hurting his eyes yet more intensely, and when they tried to walk him a few steps into the shade he swayed from side to side as alarmingly as if he was crossing the Niagara Falls on a tight-rope.

The minutes went by. The three of them stood round the groaning victim, not knowing what to do. No help came.

Mrs Craggs began to wonder whether she should have ignored Dr Crippen and called the family physician. She tried consoling herself with the thought that the hospital had seemed to be all ready to go into action. But she knew St Margaret's was a good distance away and London traffic could be terrible.

Suddenly a resolution came into her head. Without a word to Dr Crippen or Mrs Bount she hurried off down the wide gravel path that led to the green-faced, lime-bewigged statue of Sir Hans Sloane. At it she turned left past a little pool of water-loving plants and a mounded rock garden made half of pieces of lava brought from Iceland by Sir Joseph Banks in 1776 and half of stones taken from the Tower of London. But the thought of this piece of information, once given her by Mr Bount himself and since cherished, hardly scratched at the surface of her mind now. She had a mission to fulfil.

Not far beyond the pool was the narrow band of the Order Beds devoted to the Campanulaceae.

When she reached it she stopped, cast a swift eye down its length, spotted what she wanted and ran like a stamping steam-engine along the strip of grass path that gave the gardeners access to the plants. She halted, she stooped, she put her strong-fingered, brown-backed hands firmly around a clump of little waving stalks, the flowers on them not yet out, and she tugged.

Back she raced with her booty. She found the Curator mouthing something wild about Sir Hans coming down off his pedestal to help him. Mrs Bount was standing making occasional ineffective darts towards him. Dr Crippen had gone along to the corner of the building where he could see the West Gate and catch the first signs of the team from the Poisons Unit arriving.

Concealing her handful of leaves and stems temporarily in the pocket of her flowered apron, Mrs Craggs interposed herself between the groaning Curator and his wife.

She bent low.

'Here, sir,' she whispered energetically, 'chew these. Chew

'em good, an' swaller them down.'

Fearful eyes, the pupils big as peas, looked up at her.

'What? What is … ?'

'Lobelia, sir,' Mrs Craggs said. 'What we used to call vomit weed when I was a little girl in the country, sir.'

'Yes,' said the Curator, starting up a little in his chair and looking momentarily more lucid. 'Yes. Emetic properties. Lobelia. Yes. Good.'

He seized the bundle of stalks Mrs Craggs was offering him, thrust them into his mouth and began to chew as if his life depended on it.

As perhaps it did.

* * *

But now Mrs Craggs sensed that her conversation with the Curator was beginning to arouse the curiosity of his wife. She turned away with some rapidity.

'That lot from the 'ospital,' she said loudly, 'aren't they here even yet?'

Mrs Bount was immediately galvanised into new alarm. She ran over to where Dr Crippen was on the watch. She came running back to demand whether Mrs Craggs had actually got through to the hospital.

''Course I did,' Mrs Craggs replied stolidly, keeping her wiry body firmly planted between Mrs Bount and the still feebly chewing Curator.

She wondered for how long she would be able to hide what she had done. She was under no illusion that either Mrs Bount or Dr Crippen would approve of her feeding the poison victim with something grabbed from one of the Garden's beds. She wondered, too, hardly liking to allow the thoughts to rise up, whether one or the other of the two was not at this moment delighted that help was so slow in coming. Both of them bore the poor man grudges. She could not help remembering that.

However, her fears of discovery were at once relieved by a shout from Dr Crippen at the West Gate. With Mrs Bount she turned eagerly towards the corner of the laboratory building round which they expected a whole phalanx of white-coated doctors and medical aides to appear.

But it was a phalanx of a different sort, though every bit as impressive, that did at last come round the corner. Surrounded by uniformed police constables and backed by half a dozen men carrying weighty boxes of equipment, there strode into the Garden a sharp-faced, sharp-suited man already flicking quick assessing glances to left and right. Just a step behind him there came a lugubrious-looking individual wearing a suit that was by contrast startlingly baggy and grease-stained.

'Mrs Craggs? Mrs Craggs? Which one of you is Mrs Craggs?' the sharp-faced leader called out as they approached.

'I'm Mrs Craggs. An' who are you?'

For a moment the police squad leader was checked. But it was for a moment only.

'I am Detective-Superintendent Greenforest,' he announced in briskly clipped tones. 'Investigating the probable poisoning of a Mr Bount, Curator of the Physic Garden, as I understand it.'

'Yes,' said Mrs Craggs. 'An' since you understand it from me over the phone, I'm glad you've got it right.'

It was not an auspicious beginning. Nor did anything that followed go much better as it became clear that both Mrs Bount and Dr Crippen would have preferred the new arrivals to be doctors, not investigators. However, equipment of all sorts was rapidly deployed under the energetic instructions of Superintendent Greenforest, and some rather more casual questions were asked by his baggy-suited assistant, one Detective-Sergeant Gribe.

Everywhere was soon activity. Constables were posted, uselessly, at the Garden's locked gates. Others inquired, respectfully, the names of the handful of people wandering learnedly about among the plants and flowers. Yet others checked, brusquely, a roll-call of the blue-jeaned gardeners. Superintendent Greenforest conducted, sharply, a number of short interviews. His lugubrious sergeant entered various facts in a grubby notebook. Only at one place was there a marked lack of action – round the canvas chair where, in the shade, the poisoned victim still groaned painful breath after painful breath.

Superintendent Greenforest, after ascertaining that the Curator was not conceivably in a fit state to aid the inquiry, had then – Mrs Craggs thought it was in rather a hurried way – left the scene. Dr Crippen continued to hover near the West Gate looking for his pet Poisons Unit team. Mrs Bount dabbed from time to time at her husband's sweaty forehead with tissues from a large box she had ever ready for use.

Mrs Craggs paced up and down near by, feeling decidedly anxious. Every now and again she glanced over the Campanulaceae section of the Order Beds, as if to make sure that there really had been a small plant there now torn from its roots.

The minutes went inexorably by, and still there was no sign of the arrival of 'The Team'.

At last Mrs Craggs could bear it no longer. If she went on watching over poor Mr Bount, she felt, it would bring about the very opposite of what she hoped for. At just that moment of decision she spotted Superintendent Greenforest marching his baggy-suited sergeant away towards the far end of the Garden with the evident intention of discussing progress. Without hesitation she set off, as rapidly as she could, down along a parallel path, determined to hear as much as she could of what they had to say to each other. She had, in answering questions, done her best to put Sergeant Gribe wise to all the facts of the matter. She very much wanted to know if the various messages she had attempted to plant in his mind were going to get passed on.

She succeeded in installing herself very nicely under the deep-green shade of a tent-like *Fagus sylvatica* down by the path along which the two detectives were pacing in conclave. There she stood, cocking an ear like an acquisitive sparrow, and hoped to pick up crumbs.

'Yes,' she heard the superintendent say, 'a complex business, no doubt about that. Plenty of scientific knowledge involved, obviously. What it'll come down to in the end is showing our resources are superior to the murderer's.'

'If you ask me,' his sergeant replied, mournful as a bloodhound, 'it's a strict case of churchezz lar fem. I been on more than a hundred murders in my time, and it's been a family job in ninety-nine of 'em.'

'Well, it's hardly likely to be that here.' The sharp tones of the superintendent came floating over to Mrs Craggs. 'Altogether too well calculated. It's premeditation and a considerable knowledge of toxic pathology we've got to look out for here. Of course, we're lucky in that access to the Garden is limited, all those locked gates, very convenient. And there aren't so many possibilities when it comes to access to that cup of herb tea either. Not much more than a handful of gardeners and the odd visitor or two. You have noted all their names, haven't you, Sergeant? That old gent there with the white beard, talking to the lady in the macintosh. Got him?'

Sergeant Gribe heaved a sigh. A sigh loud enough for Mrs Craggs clearly to hear.

'Yes, sir,' he said. 'I do know the routine. I have done it all before.'

'All right, we'll eliminate them in due course. But I tell you frankly, Sergeant, I don't think we're going to have all that far to look when it comes down to it. It's a question of having the necessary expertise, and I think I know just where that is.'

'You don't mean that Dr Crippen?' Sergeant Gribe said, in open disbelief.

'It's the obvious possibility, Sergeant. There's motive, you know. The fellow wanted Bount's job. It didn't take me very long to find that out.'

Mrs Craggs saw the sergeant shake his bloodhound cheeks with baleful incredulity.

'Not another Crippen murderer,' he said. 'It can't happen. It just couldn't happen. Stands to reason.'

'Don't talk nonsense, man. If that's the sort of logic you're going to bring to the case you might as well go home.'

'I've been assigned to you,' Sergeant Gribe answered. 'Sir.'

It was the superintendent's turn to sigh now. Mrs Craggs thought he would blow the petals off the cascading flowers of a wild rose that grew just opposite her hiding-place, a relic doubtless of the ancient former curator's *laissez-faire* attitude.

'And if it's logic you want,' the sergeant continued heavily. 'I happen to have learned a thing or two about lar Bount. Got it from that chatterbox of a cleaning lady. Nothing in her head but talk.'

Mrs Craggs held tightly on to the trunk of the *Fagus sylvatica* to prevent herself leaping from her place of concealment.

'Yes, Madam don't like her new house,' the sergeant continued. 'Hates it, come to that. Thinks it's a danger to her kiddies. And Sir won't move. Wants to end his days here. So, if it's motive you want, you haven't got far to look, not in my book.'

The superintendent snorted with disgust.

And Mrs Craggs, behind her safe screen of drooping, ground-touching branches, snorted a moment later too. Because she saw then, in one illuminating flash, that both the theories she had overheard were quite, quite wrong. And in that same micro-second of time she had even made a reasoned guess at who the actual murderer might be.

*　*　*

She snorted so loudly that her hiding-place might well have been at that moment discovered.

Except that at the very same instant there came from up at the other end of the Garden a piercing, ululating, full-voiced scream.

The two policemen set off at a pounding run. Mrs Craggs, though not so scissoring of leg, managed somehow to be not far behind them.

They arrived, all three panting, at the place where the death's-door Curator lay. What they had expected to see defies conjecture. Mr Bount finally dead in a new extreme of agony? A second victim to add to the mystery? A wild orang-utan descending from the magnificent black mulberry tree near by?

What they did see was Mrs Bount standing with her mouth still wide open, though now voiceless, and her husband leaning forward in his chair having just voided the contents of his stomach on to the ancient paving-stones with a startling comprehensiveness.

'Oh, lor,' said Mrs Craggs. 'Me old vomit weed. It's worked at last.'

She felt fairly pleased with herself. Mr Bount, though he looked so pale his features hardly seemed to be there on his face, appeared distinctly less agitated and even to be breathing more easily.

But to his wife the abrupt alteration in his condition seemed to indicate not the beginnings of recovery but the imminence of the end.

'Roger,' she sobbed, flinging herself on to her knees beside him, 'Roger, don't leave me. Don't die, Roger.'

Mrs Craggs saw Superintendent Greenforest give Sergeant Gribe a triumphant look, a look that said plainly, 'And you thought she had tried to kill him, you crass idiot.' And she saw the malevolent glance the superintendent received from the sergeant, a glance that said with equal clarity, 'If you believe this piece of ham acting, you'll believe anything. Sir.'

But suddenly Mrs Bount turned away from her wan-faced husband. She lunged to her feet, looking wildly all around, found the person she sought and took two tottering steps towards him.

It was Dr Crippen.

'You,' she shouted, her voice ringing round the green vistas of the Garden, 'you. You did this to him. You murderer. You vile murderer. You wanted to lord it over the Garden. You always did. It was gall to you when Roger got the post. Gall. Wormwood. And now you've poisoned him. Poisoned him so that you can take over and regiment the whole place to your crazy schemes.'

Mrs Craggs, out of the corner of her eye, saw the faintest possible expression of complacent agreement steal over the youthfully alert countenance of Superintendent Greenforest.

She hardly had time to register it. Because, if Mrs Bount had attacked Dr Crippen with vehement savagery, Dr Crippen was quite as quick to return the attack with interest.

'I don't attempt to disguise the fact that Bount and I disagreed on policy,' he retorted, each word sharp as a spine of the insect-warding *Dipsacus sylvestris*, the teazel plant. 'Yet I would hardly go to the length of murder to settle our differences. On the other hand, however, I can well imagine that a wife who feels all her wishes for the future have been thwarted might well decide that she had a right to dispose of her husband – by whatever convenient means came to hand.'

From Sergeant Gribe a little grunt of satisfaction. From Superintendent Greenforest a quick 'Pah' of disbelief. But from neither one nor the other was there any move to preserve the Queen's rapidly deteriorating peace.

Mrs Craggs decided the time had come for her to put her oar in.

'You're both o' you wrong,' she announced. 'Both o' you letting silly ideas buzz round in your 'eads like blessed bluebottles.'

She saw the two detectives turning towards her as if they were ready to silence this heretical outburst by whatever means first came to hand. She plunged rapidly on.

'D'you really think,' she said to Dr Crippen, 'that if Mrs Bount here had decided to poison her hubby she'd of used some ancient old stuff what grows here in the Garden? Mrs Bount, what swears by newfangled tea-bags and latest-edition vacuum-cleaners? Nah, she'd of got hold of the very newest in the poison line. Something modern an' scientific. This ain't a Mrs Bount murder, chum, you can take my word for that.'

This last observation she addressed rather more to Sergeant Gribe than to Dr Crippen. But if it gave any pleasure to Superintendent Greenforest, it was a pleasure soon obliterated.

Mrs Craggs turned now to the Curator's wife.

'An' you're every bit as bad,' she said. 'You know that old Appointments Board turned down Dr Crippen 'cos they didn't want the Garden made into some sort o' 'ygienic laboratory. You knew they wasn't never going to make him Curator however many times your old hubby popped off. You knew it, an' so did Dr Crippen. So he wasn't never going to commit no murder.'

'But,' said Superintendent Greenforest, shocked into involuntary speech, 'but if Dr Crippen didn't – and if Mrs Bount – well, who then? Who?'

'Well, I ain't got no proof, mind,' Mrs Craggs said. 'But all the same, dear, just take a look over there.'

She extended a wiry, brown-skinned, naked-to-the-elbow arm in the direction of the distant, elegant Chinese willow-pattern tree. But her jabbing, pointing finger indicated a less beautiful object within easy hearing distance of the group of them, a somewhat elderly greenhouse. And at its corner was a figure, plainly lurking, dressed in an enveloping dull-grey macintosh with a matching dull-grey round hat.

'I dunno,' she said, 'but I saw that one once putting back a few little plants what Mr Bount ordered to be grubbed up 'cos there was too many of 'em. Now that was a sign o' madness, if you like.'

'Why, yes, of course,' Dr Crippen said. 'That's old Miss Macadam. Quite a good amateur botanist, in her way, but she's been mad as a hatter for years. Everybody knows that.'

Everybody except me, thought Mrs Craggs. She pursed her lips in resignation.

'Yes,' old Miss Macadam suddenly yelled from beside the greenhouse, 'yes, yes, yes. He had to go. Had to go. Pulling up my favourites. One after the other. The man was a vandal. He had to go.'

Superintendent Greenforest, faithfully flanked by Sergeant Gribe, advanced.

'Well,' a quiet voice said from behind them, 'one does have to make a few changes, you know. One really does.'

171

They turned. Mr Bount was sitting up in his chair and looking very much more cheerful.

It was a cheerfulness he succeeded in retaining even when at that very moment the Poisons Unit team from St Margaret's Hospital arrived in all its glory and promptly began to subject him to a series of on-the-spot tests.

'You know, all this is hardly necessary,' he remarked as soon as the thermometer had been removed from his mouth. 'We all know what happened to me. A cupful of a good old traditional poison, quite quickly followed by a good old-fashioned dose of physic. It's all ended happily. Thanks to Mrs Craggs.'

WELL, I think that's about all, Mrs Milhorne. Thank —
    Yaiss, she's a funny old thing, reely, Elma Craggs. I
mean, she ain't what you might call modern at all. Not
like what I am, if you take my meaning. Well, you got to
keep up to date, haven't you? But Elma. Never a bit. Not
one wink. All the old things, it's them what she – it is
those there that what she is attracted to. Yaiss. All the old
stuff. Nothing nice an' modern an' refined.

XI

MRS CRAGGS AND THE ROUND BLUE
IMMORTALS

THE GREATER LONDON COUNCIL WIELDED in its day almost as much power as many of the smaller nations of the world. It even had the right to confer immortality.

This, however, it generously devolved upon one of its lesser sub-committees, its Historic Buildings Board. At its monthly meetings the Board, besides listing for preservation against the fury of the property developers close on 30,000 of London's architectural memorabilia, used to decide which of the city's former inhabitants should be commemorated in perpetuity – or as near as damn it – by having a ceramic plaque in an attractive shade of blue erected to their memory on a house in which at some time they dwelt. There are in all some 370 such plaques, and two of them are where they are owing to the determined advocacy of Mrs Craggs.

How this came to be is a complicated story. But then, as Mrs Craggs frequently remarks to Mrs Milhorne, 'Life ain't exactly no bowl o' roses, more of a garden what no one's had the time to go gardenin' in.' And Mrs Craggs can spot a weed if it sprouts up under her face rather quicker than most.

When Mrs Craggs was one of the army of ladies responsible for keeping in good array the massive pile of County Hall looking northwards over the wide-flowing Thames by

Westminster Bridge she encountered early one afternoon a chap in a long brown overall, evidently one of the caretaking corps whom she had never chanced to meet before. And immediately he addressed her.

''Ere, love, you ain't got a broom you could give us a lend of, 'ave you?'

Mrs Craggs reflected that, since she was in fact carrying a broom, this was not the most pertinent of questions. Besides, there was something about the caretaker – it may have been his big black curly moustache which looked as if it had been stuck on only that morning, or it may have been his eyes which although they were large and brown and dog-like still had a way of flicking from side to side which was at least disconcerting – that made her wonder. But she agreed to lend her broom nevertheless. She believed that you have got to show a bit of trust yourself or no one will ever trust you.

Yet, as the fellow turned away after the transaction was completed – rather quickly, Mrs Craggs thought – she was prompted to ask him his name, with just a touch of sharpness.

'Name? Name?' He seemed quite bewildered. 'Oh, my name. It's – er – Gumshoe. Mr Gumshoe.'

'All right, Mr Gumshoe,' Mrs Craggs said, giving him a bit of a smile. 'An' you will remember that broom's me own particular, won't you, an' put it back in me little cupboard, in Conference Room 17, right down the far end next to the pillar?'

'I will,' said Mr Gumshoe, and went with the broom straight into that very room.

Gumshoe, Mrs Craggs mused. That's a funny old sort of a monniker all right. Sounds like one o' them American private-eyes or something. Well, maybe that's what 'is great-great-grandfather was. You never can tell.

And she thought no more about it, except to hope a little later on that Mr Gumshoe had closed the door of her private cupboard properly since Conference Room 17 was being used that afternoon for the monthly meeting of the Historic Buildings Board. Then, shortly before she was due to finish for the day, the Cleaning and Maintenance Supervisor came rushing up to her. And she could see at once that he was in a taking.

'Mrs Craggs, Mrs Craggs, just the person.'

'Oh, yes?'

'Mrs Craggs, Rest and Refreshment Room No 32, it's been disgracefully neglected' – Mrs Milhorne, thought Mrs Craggs, had another of her turns, but why don't she never tell me? – 'and, Mrs Craggs, the Brooms and Ancillary Equipment Store is locked up now and you're the only one with access to a sweeping instrument. Your very own broom, Mrs Craggs. Irregular, of course, but a godsend now. A godsend.'

''Cept it's in a cupboard just where that old Historic Buildings Board is at it 'ammer an' tongs,' said Mrs Craggs.

'Oh, dear diddle-dee me. Oh dear, oh dear. But, no. No, there's nothing else for it. You see, the Board takes tea in No 32. No, you'll have to go in and fetch your broom. But, oh, Mrs Craggs, be quiet, won't you, please. A veritable mouse, Mrs Craggs.'

Mrs Craggs was not quiet. If you got a shoe what creaks, you got a shoe what creaks, she thought as she made her way right down the side of the conference room to the little discreet unofficial cupboard where she kept her very own broom, one you could rely on to make a decent job of things. But the squeaking hardly mattered: the Board was indeed at it hammer and tongs. They were discussing whether or not to put on the preservation list somewhere called Mulcaster House. Mrs Craggs could not help hearing. As she said to Mrs Milhorne afterwards, 'You couldn't no more have not heard as you could of kept out the water if so be as you took a stroll under the Niagary Falls.' The point at issue seemed to be whether or not a plaque on the building commemorating Herbert Mulcaster, originator of the Penny Tramway, was enough to save it. And Councillor Pumpleton, never a favourite with Mrs Craggs since he had once addressed her as 'my good woman', was booming and thundering about how it was high time every one of these appalling old places was razed to the ground, 'to the ground'.

And Sir James Bennyson, the Master of the Queen's Poesy, who came to the Board as an adviser, at the single mention of plaques had started in his high hooting voice to beg them to 'get on to the interesting bit, I mean who shall we put up on the walls.' So one way and another the room was verging on the cacophanous, and Mrs Craggs got to her cupboard unnoticed.

Only, when she opened it, she had rather a surprise. Mr Gumshoe had put her broom back there all right, but he had also put himself in the little confined space along with the broom.

Mrs Craggs looked at him, and he looked at Mrs Craggs, his big brown doggy eyes taking on an expression of extreme piteousness. And all the while behind them the debate went on, torrentially.

Then just as Mrs Craggs had made up her mind that, despite the tendency of those piteous dog-eyes still to flick this way and that, she would say nothing at all about Mr Gumshoe's curious presence in her broom cupboard – after all, funny though it was, she never had gone much on tittle-tattling on a fellow-worker – evidently the Board came to some sort of a decision. 'All right, Sir James, all right,' she heard the Chairman say, 'since there seems to be general agreement that Mulcaster House will have to go, let's move on to "plaques".' 'Oh, hooray, hooray,' hooted Sir James, and Mrs Craggs thought that it was nice to hear someone being happy and excited about something, even if the old boy did get a bit above himself at times.

So she set off, with her broom, back towards the door, having to take it slowly so as to keep to the minimum the infuriated-oboe squeaks of her shoe. And in this way she heard a good deal of that day's preliminary discussion about who might be commemorated for ever on round blue plaques. And pretty silly she thought most of the suggestions were. Cor, she said to herself, why don't they pick on someone what's done some good to people, like that old Herbert Mulcaster with his Penny Tramway or, more to the point, Josiah Sprague. Mrs

Craggs knew about Josiah Sprague because only three doors along from her own home was the house where he had spent all his days, as well as inventing the Snippo fastener, a tiny but immensely useful device for which Mrs Craggs and countless other ladies both high and low had had tremendous cause to be grateful.

She was still thinking about old Josiah Sprague and all the good his invention had done over the seventy years and more it had been in existence when it was borne in on her that the Historic Buildings Board was no longer considering blue plaques but was instead considering her.

'Mr Chairman,' Councillor Pumpleton was thundering, 'I insist that that woman be removed. Absorbing and overhearing the highly important and confidential discussions of this committee. It is nothing short of scandalous.'

It was the words 'that woman' that did it. Otherwise Mrs Craggs might have explained as well as she could and apologised and scuttled out. But there were some things she was not going to stand for.

'That woman, indeed,' she said, coming and planting herself directly in front of Councillor Pumpleton. 'Important discussions, indeed. Nothing but a lot of tommyrot, as well you know. Putting up plaques to music-hall comedians what no one ain't never heard of an' poets what spent all their money on drink an' didn't leave theirself the price of bed-and-breakfast regular. Tommyrot from first to last. And not a word of a plaque for poor old Josiah Sprague.'

It looked as though Councillor Pumpleton, whose face was in any case rather red and fat, was going to explode from apoplexy. But it was not his voice that broke the silence. It was that of the Master of the Queen's Poesy. 'Josiah Sprague,' he said. 'Inventor of the Snippo. Jolly good idea. Deserves a plaque if anyone ever did. Pity there won't be any written records of house occupation, though. Got to have those, you know.'

'Oh, no, you ain't,' said Mrs Craggs who was, as she later told Mrs Milhorne, fair swept away by now.

'But, dear lady,' said Sir James. 'I'm sadly afraid evidence is absolutely necessary.'

Mrs Craggs shook her head from side to side.

'That's just what I got,' she answered. 'Old Man Pettiforth. 'Ow about him? What better evidence can you have than a feller that lived in the selfsame house an' what's a hundred years old, telegram from the Queen an' all?'

'Well, yes,' said the Master of Poesy. 'Yes, what better indeed? Gentlemen, I propose Josiah Sprague.'

'Nonsense,' bawled Councillor Pumpleton. 'Inventor of some tuppenny-ha'penny fastener. The ratepayers will riot. Red blood-running riot, I tell you.'

'Tuppenny ha'penny?' Mrs Craggs rounded on him. 'What you know about it? Them fasteners was never tuppence ha'penny. Penny farthing they was, if they was that. A regular benefactor was old Josiah. Just like that Herbert Mulcaster an' the Penny Tramway what you was the one as wanted to pull down.'

And even as she said these words, and even as Councillor Pumpleton thundered and blasted against her as she knew he would, an idea came sweeping into Mrs Craggs's head like a great white dawn flooding over the darkened countryside.

'An' what's more,' she interrupted the councillor in full spate. 'What's more, I dare say there's a good deal more to knocking down that old Mulcaster House than meets the eye. A good deal more.'

She had the satisfaction then of seeing Councillor Pumpleton checked in mid-flow, of seeing him suddenly look considerably thoughtful and a little bit afraid.

'What do you mean, woman?' he snapped. 'We shall all be together taking tea next door after the meeting. No one will have access to a telephone. There's nothing anyone can prove.'

'Oh, yes, there is,' said Mrs Craggs.

She swept round and marched straight back down the room to the little half-concealed cupboard where she liked to keep her own private broom and when she got to it she flung wide its door. And there, looking like a very much ashamed dog caught with the joint in its jaws, was Mr Gumshoe, who cast one furious glance at Councillor Pumpleton and scuttled from the room, tail between his legs.

'Well now,' said Mrs Craggs. 'What if there was a prime site somewhere and a nice old building on it? An' what if this 'ere Committee or Board, or whatever it is, said as they'd allow that building to be demolished? Lot o' money it'd be worth then to one o' those what they call property developers if as how they got to know about that this very afternoon before no one else. And what if there was someone who hid hisself just so as to hear the decision and give it out before any member of the committee possibly could? Then there'd be something to call scandalous, there would then.'

'So there jolly well would,' said Sir James. 'And do you know, Mr Chairman, I don't think a proper vote was ever taken on Mulcaster House. So wouldn't it be a good thing to take one now?'

And they did. And there was no one at all who voted in favour of demolition (Councillor Pumpleton abstained). And then they voted on a plaque to old Josiah Sprague and there was no one at all who voted against that (Councillor Pumpleton had left the room). So sometimes Mrs Craggs goes for a walk that takes her past Mulcaster House and its blue plaque as well as the one just three doors along from her own home, and she looks up at each of them and doesn't say a word. But there's a gleam in her eye.

*Well, Mrs Milhorne, I think I must be off now. There's a
tremendous lot —*

You know, I ain't ever – I haven't never thought o' this
before, but old Elma, she's funny reely. I don't mean
funny to make you laugh. I don't think some of the things
she says are reely very nice at all. But she's funny in her
ways, if you get my meaning. She's funny in what she'll do
and who she thinks she'll do it for. I mean, we'd all of us
go out of our way to help somebody as reely deserves it. I
mean, like I'm helping the television now. Someone reely
nice and sort of important, if you get my meaning. But
Elma ...

XII

MRS CRAGGS AND A SAD CASE OF SIMONY

THE CHURCH OF ST JAMES THE LESS, Westminster, occupies only a comparatively modest place among the ecclesiastical delights of London. Yet it is not without its claims. Built between 1860 and 1861, at the cost of the Misses Monk in memory of their father, a former Bishop of Gloucester and Bristol, it was the first religious work in London of the designer, G.E. Street. In its bold brickwork relieved by bands of sooty black and its four-square belfry tower capped by a sturdy slate-hung spire and four echoing spirelets it embodies all the confident vigour of the High Victorian together with a unity of scale that makes it an unassertive work of art. Mrs Craggs, in her short acquaintance with the building came to feel for it a strong affection. You could almost have called it love.

Which was, no doubt, why the startling events in its life she was herself responsible for so much upset her, even though her connection with the place lasted no more than three weeks.

At whatever date it may have been that she was employed at the church, which nowadays is merely a junior partner to nearby St Saviour's, it then had its own rector, its own curate and its own churchwardens assisted by their own sidesman. It was to this last that Mrs Craggs owed her temporary appointment. Up to that year Mr Breckinshaw himself had during the summer holiday period, when the volunteer cleaners from among the humbler members of the flock were away, taken over their task.

But now, as the Rector explained to Mrs Craggs, certain increased responsibilities outside the life of the parish – the Rector was a little uncertain about the exact nature of Mr Breckinshaw's employment – meant that the sidesman could not set the church to rights on Monday mornings after its Sunday use.

'So, my dear lady, since you are happily available, we would be delighted – yes, positively delighted – if you would assist us. At, of course, the customary rate of remuneration. We are not, alas, a wealthy parish – a small dole only in the collection bag each week I'm afraid, sometimes indeed not exceeding five pounds – but for this short time we can – er – manage. Yes, manage.'

'Thank you, sir,' said Mrs Craggs firmly.

The arrangement, though she had no doubt it was altogether imprecise in the Rector's mind, suited her well. She had already seen the inside of the church and she ached to give a really good polish to its long brass altar rail, to the tall narrow brass pillars round the font, to the brass eagle of the reading-stand and, most of all, to the big, plump-bellied brass ewer used for christenings. And she liked the old Rector, too. He had such clean hands, pink as a new-bathed baby's, as he had twiddled and twirled his fingers while they had discussed – without any figure ever being mentioned – the delicate matter of her pay.

The curate, when she met him on the first Monday on which, in place of Mr Breckinshaw called away to higher things, she set to with broom and duster, polishing rag and Brasso, she did not like so much. He was, naturally, a youngish man, but to her eye he was without that moderate belief in his own abilities that even a youngish man ought to have. And his unsureness took the form of making jokes.

'Ah, ha. It's – hum – Miss Craggs, isn't it? Ah, yes, Miss

Craggs. And how does it go, hm? How does it go, the sweeping and the – ha, hum, the rest?'

He did not wait for an answer.

Mrs Craggs thought about correcting him over the matter of her marital status. But decided that he wouldn't remember if she did.

'Ha, yes, Miss Craggs,' he went nervously on as he returned. 'To each his appointed task, hm? You to wafting away the – hum – dust and collecting up the – ha, hum – hassocks, and me to hearing the occasional confession of the dreadful sins of our little parish, hey? The sad cases of – ha, hum – simony. Yes, shall we say simony? Simony rife in the parish, Miss Craggs. Ho, hum, yes.'

And off he swept again, the skirts of his cassock – for this was a particularly High Anglican parish in those days – swishing like an actor's cloak as he made his way up the chancel under the huge painting, by G.F. Watts no less, of substantial angels praising the Almighty as they rest firmly on pale golden clouds (these reminded Mrs Craggs, irresistibly, of éclair pastry).

With a sigh, Mrs Craggs decided that for this week she would have to postpone taking a good feather duster to the tops of the browny-red polished granite pillars where, half-hidden amid vigorous stone foliage, there lurked little stone pictures named as such scenes as 'A Sower went forth ...', 'He selleth all that he hath ...' and 'Cut it down ...' The sweeping had been scandalously neglected by the volunteers and it would take her all her time to put things right.

But when the Rector at the end of her morning's work thrust into her hand in exchange for the key of the church a small brown coin-clinking envelope – Mr Breckinshaw must have told him how much to put in it, she thought – she took the opportunity of asking him just what simony was. It had worried her ever since the curate had used the word, and she knew that the Rector would not mind explaining. He had already told her why it was that the church's patron saint had his rather curious name.

'I mean sir,' she had said at their first interview, 'the Less.

187

It's a funny old monniker, you can't deny.'

The Rector's bland face had shown a momentary look of surprise at her question and his plump pink fingers had knotted themselves up almost inextricably. But not for long.

'Well, yes, Mrs Craggs, but one must suppose that if the dear saint appears to be in a somewhat inferior position, then he is content with it. Content with his station. And that, of course, is not necessarily the lowest. Perhaps you don't know of all the other Saint Jameses. James the Apostle first of all, of course. He's St James the Greater, I believe. His bones are said to lie at Compostella in Spain, a great centre of pilgrimage. Then, let me see. There's St James Deacon, and St James of Nisibus ...' A clean, clean hand wandered to the close-packed ranks of books on the shelves behind him and plucked down a volume. 'Yes, and there's the St James after whom one puts, in brackets, "Tarantaise", and St James Intercisus and, of course, St James the Penitent. A goodly company. With our James in his place in it.'

'Yes, I likes that, sir,' Mrs Craggs had said. 'I really does. I mean, it's better, ain't it, than wanting to be the Most, an' better too, if you ask me, than going on and on about being the Least.'

She had thought then for a moment that if she ended up as a saint – and she had no more idea of doing so than of ending up as Chancellor of the Duchy of Lancaster – then she'd settle very happily for being Saint Elma the Less.

'Now, I wonder, dear lady,' the Rector had said then, 'would you consider it an impertinence, when it comes to our patronal festival again, if I were to preach upon the subject you have so happily brought to my mind. On being content to be the Less. Yes. Yes, not without its relevance to our times, I venture to think. Not without its relevance.'

So now, standing in the well-proportioned cloister that links the church itself to its four-square belfry tower, Mrs Craggs did not hesitate to ask this other question.

'Excuse me, sir, but could you tell me something? What exactly's simony, sir?'

188

'Simony? Simony, my dear lady?'

The Rector's pink fingers locked, and after a moment unlocked.

'Well, simony, since you ask, is generally defined as – er – the buying and selling of ecclesiastical preferment. Something of that sort.'

'Yes, sir.'

Mrs Craggs buttoned her faded cherry-red macintosh across her flowered apron.

'And ecclesi-whatsit, sir?' she asked. 'And preferment?'

'Ah, dear me, yes. What fearful jargon we find ourselves betrayed into using. Yes. Well, shall we say, "to do with the church" and "getting a better job". Yes, I think that's about right.'

'Thank you very much, sir. An' see you Monday next, same time.'

'Yes. Yes, thank you, Mrs Craggs. Er – thank you.'

But, little though the Rector knew it, simony was before long to raise its head in his quiet parish. And Mrs Craggs, thanks to the clue of the forty-nine hassocks, was to be the one who would cause it so unexpectedly to rear up.

It was that next Monday, the second of the three during which Mrs Craggs brought her unflagging elbows to the Church of St James the Less, that the clue came to her attention. Before beginning to sweep she had gone systematically along the pews picking up each used hassock from where the day before prayerful knees had implanted it, and restoring it to its place leaning up against the back of the pew in front. And as she picked up and straightened she had counted: ... eight, nine, ten ... twenty-five, twenty-six ... forty-seven, forty-eight, forty-nine.

'Forty-nine of 'em at it yesterday then,' she concluded, her cheerful whisper soon lost in the airy space underneath the gold-star-painted wooden roof. 'That ain't so bad, not for these days. Though you might —'

She broke off abruptly as, with a swish and crack of cassock skirts that would have done credit to a racing yacht about to

189

bag the America's Cup, the curate came in.

'Ah, Miss – Miss – ho, hum, yes. Yes, Miss Craggs. Good morning to you. I see Mr Breckinshaw's advowson is still working in your favour. Ho, hum, yes.'

And, before Mrs Craggs had had time to wish him good day in return, he had marched away up to the altar, bobbed down on one knee, made a sign of the cross that rather resembled the gesture of an over-excited Spanish traffic policeman and plunged off to some mysterious task at the side altar.

Mrs Craggs fetched her broom and began sweeping, doing her best to forget whatever silly word the curate had used to her, so as not to have to bother the old Rector with more questions. Indeed, she succeeded in forgetting too, so vigorously did she sweep, what had just come into her mind as she had counted the forty-ninth hassock.

It was only when, coming out of the public bar at the Lord High Admiral, which stands conveniently next to the church, where she had disbursed on brown ale a small part of the contents of the brown envelope the Rector had put into her hand, she happened to see Mr Breckinshaw, very smart in a new-looking blue suit, about to go into the pub's saloon bar, that the thought of the hassocks came back to her.

'Mr Breckinshaw, Mr Breckinshaw,' she called out before she had had much time to think.

That gentleman turned at the sound of his name and inclined his head – he had a truly flourishing curvy moustache – towards Mrs Craggs in token of recognition.

She went tramping up to him.

'Oh, Mr Breckinshaw,' she said. 'Good job I saw you. You know what I gone an' done? Left me good pair o' shoes in the back o' the church there, an' the Rector's got the key again now. I don't suppose you have a set of your own, do you?'

Mr Breckinshaw considered for a moment or two.

'Why, yes, Mrs Craggs,' he answered at last. 'I do 'ave a key, as a matter of fact. My responsibilities entitle me. My growing responsibilities.'

190

He extracted the key from a pocket of his new blue suit and handed it over.

'You will find me in the Saloon Bar,' he said. 'Please return the key without fail. It's necessary to me, you know. Necessary.'

'Without fail, Mr Breckinshaw,' Mrs Craggs said.

And back she went into the locked and now deserted church. But there she wasted no time looking for a non-existent pair of good shoes. Instead she poked round in the back recesses of the nave where items necessary to the performance of the services were kept, stacks of *Hymns Ancient and Modern*, the processional cross, the choirboys' bright red cassocks and snowy-white surplices.

She left deep in thought. But not so deep that she neglected to penetrate into the social upper reaches of the Lord High Admiral and there hand back to Mr Breckinshaw his key – 'Thank you, Mrs Craggs, my duties, you know' – safe in the belief that he would fail to notice she was still wearing the same shoes.

Her state of particular thoughtfulness was renewed the following Monday, the last of the three on which she was to enjoy the solid workmanship and unassertive beauty of St James the Less, when once again she collected up the used hassocks. Only forty-eight this time, but she reckoned a good enough tally for the holiday season.

And, once again, her thoughts were interrupted by the arrival of the curate, cassock flapping as if it led a hectic life of its own.

'Hah, Miss Craggs. Once more into the breach, eh? But not, I fear, in this parish into the – ho, hum – breeches. Our good Rector does not subscribe very strongly to the Church's wish to give womanhood a greater share in its affairs. A certain democratisation, yes, but only – ho, hum – for us males.'

Mrs Craggs, leaving to fetch her broom from the rear of the building among the cassocks and surplices, the *Hymns Ancient and Modern* and the dark velvet collection bag, decided that the curate would not notice whether she had replied to all the words he had tumbled out or not.

No more did she feel obliged to respond to the second instalment she received as he swished past her again on his way out.

'Yes, yes, Miss Craggs. Democracy the keynote nowadays. *La carrière ouverte aux talents*, you know. Ho, hum, yes. And Mr Breckinshaw to take tea this afternoon with the Rector, instead of it being the other way about as it has been more than once recently, for all his comparatively low station in life – ho, hum, yes. And to be asked to become Rector's Warden, no less. Ho, hum. In succession to the late Sir Hubert Palliser. Yes, *ouverte aux talents* indeed.'

Mrs Craggs's first reaction to all that was to think that she must be going barmy. She hadn't understood a word. But then she realised that she had understood something. One or two things at least.

She saw to it that she left the brass altar rail, the brass font pillars, the brass eagle reading-stand and the brass christening ewer shining as they had not shone for years, and then, looking even more thoughtful than before, she went to hand back the church key to the Rector.

When he saw her his mild white eyebrows rose involuntarily.

'Why, Mrs Craggs, you look — Dear me, you look, if I may say so, not unlike the Angel of Wrath. Is there anything the matter?'

'There is, sir,' said Mrs Craggs. 'It's a case o' simony, I'm sorry to have to tell you. A nasty case o' simony.'

'Oh, dear, oh dear. Simony, you say, Mrs Craggs? You're sure?'

'Pretty well, sir, pretty well. Otherwise I wouldn't have spoke.'

The Rector looked looked at her, blue eyes less twinkling now under snowy eyebrows.

'No, Mrs Craggs, I rather think you wouldn't. So what exactly is it all about?'

'The hassocks, sir. That's where it began.'

'The hassocks, Mrs Craggs? And – er – simony?'

'I reckon so, sir. You see, I don't suppose as you've got

192

much of a 'ead for figures, have you?'

'Why, no, Mrs Craggs. One of my failings, alas.'

'Thought so, sir, from the way you couldn't say how much I was to have for me three hours of a Monday. An' that curate … Well, meaning no disrespec', but it's plain as plain he thinks as he's got more to think about than five quid in the little money-bag what's passed round of a Sunday.'

'Mrs Craggs, I'm lost, I'm afraid. Quite lost.'

'Well, who's to blame you, sir? But some things is clear enough if you looks in the right direction. An' some of 'em's that forty-nine hassocks, call it fifty, an' five quid in total is no more'n two bob a head. An' you don't mean to tell me, sir, that people like that Sir Hubert didn't dish up more'n a couple of bob.'

'Well, yes, Mrs Craggs. I'm sure you're right. A good many of my parishioners are not without their share of the world's goods, and some almost certainly put a pound note into the bag each Sunday.'

A bewildered look of dawning understanding had appeared on his normally cheerful pink countenance.

'Mrs Craggs,' he said, 'what's been happening?'

'That's what I come to ask meself, sir. An' then, when I seen a certain sign, I decided I better have a look at that old collection bag, sir. An' I did. An' it's a two-pocket job, sir.'

'A two-pocket job?'

'Yes, sir. Someone's sewed a sort o' flap inside so that half the money goes one way an' half the other an' no one notices as they puts their ten bob or their quid in that there's a fair lot there already.'

'Yes. Yes, Mrs Craggs, I think I understand now.'

The Rector's clean, clean pink fingers mimed the necessary little manoeuvre.

'Yes, I do understand. But who, Mrs Craggs? Who?'

'Who took to asking you to tea, sir?' Mrs Craggs replied. 'Who are you going to have back this very afternoon, wearing his new blue suit, an' ask to be your churchwarden an' have his say as to what goes on? Who goes to the saloon bar in the Lord

High Admiral, sir? I'm afraid it's like what it says on one o' them little stone pictures in the church, sir. The man what found a treasure hid in a field, kept it to himself like an' sold all that he hath to buyeth the field.'

'Why, yes, Mrs Craggs, I'm afraid it is. The buying of ecclesiastical preferment. Yes, indeed. And I'm afraid, too, it will have to be a question of another of those pillar parables. "Cut it down", Mrs Craggs, "it cumbereth the ground".'

'Cumbereth's right, sir. But it's a fair pity. It's gone an' spoilt old St James the Less for me, sir. Downright spoilt it.'

Look, I'm sorry, Mrs Milhorne, but I've simply got to fly.

Yaiss, well, o' course, it's all very well going on about Elma Craggs an' her five senses. Well, I mean, we've all got those, haven't we? And don't want to think about them too much, if you ask me. I mean, smell. Not what I call very refined, is it? No, what I say is: it's the sixth sense that counts.

I'm sure. But —

Now, when it comes to a sixth sense, well, I don't want to go doing any of what you might call boasting, but I'm sure I've got as much of that as Elma Craggs, and more. Now, if you was wanting something reely interesting for your programme, I could —

No. No. Er — that is, I don't think that would quite fit, you know. And I really must —

Yaiss, yaiss, I sometimes think I must of been the seventh daughter of a seventh daughter. Not that my Mum, that my mothah, had more children than only me. Myself, I should say. But you have got to account for sensitivity somehow. Stands to reason, doesn't it?

XIII

MRS CRAGGS'S SIXTH SENSE

IT WAS A GOOD THING THAT Mrs Craggs, though still only middle-aged, had had her twinges. If she had not, and had not acted on them, to begin with the nasty little something-or-other that had developed just under the skin on her right elbow could not have been dealt with so easily, and, more important, poor old Professor Partheman would have been in much worse trouble than he was. But twinges she did have, her doctor she went to, and he recommended a very minor operation. With the consequence that Mrs Craggs 'did for' Professor Partheman that particular week on the Wednesday and not the Thursday.

And so she set eyes on Ramon.

He was doing no more than mow the lawn in front of the professor's ground-floor flat and from time to time taking a boxful of clippings round to the compost heap behind the shrubbery. But that was enough for Mrs Craggs.

'Excuse me for mentioning it, sir,' she said to the professor as she tucked her wages into her purse, 'but I would just like to say a word about that chap.'

'What chap, Mrs Craggs? I was not aware that we had discussed any chap.'

The old professor was a bit spiky and a bit silly sometimes, but Mrs Craggs liked working for him because, despite his great age, there he was every time she came, beavering away at his writing and papers, doing his job and no messing about. So she ignored the objection, and went on with what she had to say.

'That feller what you've got in to mow your old bit of a lawn, sir.'

'Ramon, Mrs Craggs,' said the professor. 'A young Spaniard employed as domestic help over at Flinwich local teacher training college and making a little extra on his day off. He's particularly pleased to come because I speak his language. Now, what do you want to say about him?'

The professor glared rather, as if he already knew without realising it that Mrs Craggs had an adverse comment to make.

'I don't think you ought to have him around, sir,' she said. 'I don't like the looks of him, and that's a fact.'

'Mrs Craggs,' said the professor in the voice he had used to put down any number of uppish undergraduates, 'that you do not "like the looks" of Ramon may be a fact, but anything else you have said or implied about him most certainly is not. Now, do you know any facts to the young man's detriment?'

'Facts, I don't know, sir. But feelings I have. He'll do you no good and of that I'm certain sure.'

'My dear good lady, are you really suggesting that I should cease to offer the fellow employment just because of some mysterious feeling you have? What is it about his looks that you don't like, for heaven's sake?'

Mrs Craggs thought. She had not up to that moment attempted to analyse her feeling. She had just had it. But overwhelmingly.

After a little she managed to pin something down.

'I think it's the way he prowls, sir,' she said. 'Whenever he goes anywhere, he prowls. Like an animal, sir. A – A –'

She searched her mind.

'A jaguar, sir. He prowls like one o' them jaguars. That's it.'

'My dear Mrs Craggs. You cannot really be telling me that all you have against the chap is the way he walks. It's too ridiculous.'

But Mrs Craggs was not so easily discouraged. She thought about the young Spanish gardener at intervals right up to the following Monday when she was next due at the professor's. She even was thinking about him during the minor operation which had been such a striking success. And when on the Monday she was given her money she broached the subject again.

'That Ramon, sir. I hope as 'ow you've had second thoughts there.'

'Second thoughts.' The aged professor's parchment-white face became suffused with pinkness. 'Let me tell you, my dear lady, I had no need for more than the swiftest of first thoughts. I have spent a lifetime dealing in facts, Mrs Craggs, good hard facts, and I'm scarcely likely to abandon them now. Not one word more, if you please.'

Mrs Craggs sighed.

'As you like, sir.'

But, though she said no more then, she made up her mind to do all that she could to protect the old professor from the jaguar she had seen prowling across his lawn carefully avoiding ever appearing to look in at the windows of the flat.

And, she thought, she had one way of perhaps obtaining some 'facts'. It so happened at that time that Mrs Milhorne was employed as a daily cleaner at the teacher training college. So at the first opportunity she paid her a visit at her home, though that was unfortunately not till the following Tuesday evening.

'Oh, yaiss, Ramon,' said Mrs Milhorne. 'I always knew in my bones about him. Handsome he may have been, and sort of romantic, if you take my meaning, but I never tried to make up to him, no matter what they say.'

'I'm sure you didn't, dear,' said Mrs Craggs, who knew her friend's susceptible nature. 'But why do you go on about him as if he ain't there no more?'

'Because that's what he ain't,' said Mrs Milhorne.

And then the whole story came out. Ramon had been dismissed about a fortnight before, suspected of having brutally attacked a young Spanish maid at the college. The girl,

Rosita by name, although battered about terribly and still actually off work, had refused to say who had caused her injuries. But, as Ramon had notoriously been attracted to her, no one really had had any doubt.

"Spect he's back in Spain now,' said Mrs Milhorne, and she sighed.

'No, he's not,' Mrs Craggs said. 'I told you, dear. He's coming every Wednesday to mow old Professor Partheman's lawn, and the professor's study's just full of picture frames all dotted with old coins, gold most of 'em. He's what's called a new-miserist. An' if that Ramon's just half o' what I think he is, he'll be planning to help himself to them coins, specially now he's out of a job.'

A red flush of excitement came up on Mrs Milhorne's pallid face.

'We'll have to go to the rescue,' she said. 'Just like on telly. The US Cavalry.'

'Yes,' said Mrs Craggs. 'Only when old Professor Partheman sees you a-galloping up, an' me come to that, you know what he'll do? He'll tell us to turn right round and gallop away again. Or he will unless we come waving some facts on our little blue flags.'

She stood considering.

'Rosita,' she said at last. 'She's got to be made to talk.'

But since Rosita, like Ramon, had hardly a word of English and since she had obstinately persevered with her silence, Mrs Craggs's plan seemed to be up against insuperable difficulties.

Only it was Mrs Craggs's plan.

Introduced next morning to the room in which Rosita was resting, her face still blotched with heavy bruises, Mrs Craggs first gave her a smile which would have warmed the heart of even a dumb animal, and then joined her in a nice cuppa, selecting from a plate of biscuits the sweetest and stickiest and pressing them on the Spanish girl with such hearty insistence that if the interview was to do nothing else it would at least add some ounces to her already deliciously buxom figure. But Mrs Craggs had only just begun.

"Ere,' she said to Rosita, when she judged the moment ripe. 'You know I works for an old professor?'

Rosita would hardly have understood this abruptly proferred piece of information had not Mrs Craggs at the same time jumped to her feet and first mimed to a T the old numismatist, frail as a branch of dried twigs, and then had imitated herself brushing and dusting and polishing fit to bust.

'*Si, si*,' said the Spanish girl, eyes alight and dancing. 'Work, *si, si*. Ol' man, *si, si*.'

'Ah, you're right, dear,' Mrs Craggs said. 'But I ain't the only one what works for him.'

Another bout of miming.

'*Ah, si. Si. Jardinero*.'

'Yes,' said Mrs Craggs. 'A gardener. Ramon.'

And, although her pronunciation was hardly one hundred per cent, the vigour she put into saying the word sent at once a wave of pallor across the Spanish girl's plump and pretty face.

'*Ah, si, Ramon*.'

'Yes, dear. You got it nicely. But listen. That old prof, he's got a lot o' coins in his study. His study, see.'

In place of Mrs Craggs there came a picture of an ancient scholar bent over his books, scribbling rapidly on sheet after sheet of paper and from time to time taking a rare and valuable old coin and scrutinising it with extraordinary care.

'*Ah, si*. He have *dinero antiguo, si*.' And then suddenly a new expression swept over her face. '*Dios*,' she said. '*Ramon*.'

After that it was the work of only half a minute for Mrs Craggs to be seated at the driving wheel of some vehicle capable of the most amazing speeds, and then to reincarnate her pictures of Professor Partheman and put on to his lips a stream of sound accompanied by many florid gestures, that could not have meant anything to anybody but made it perfectly clear that the old man was a fluent speaker of Spanish. Rosita seized a coat and scarf and showed herself ready for instant departure.

'But, hurry,' said Mrs Craggs. 'We ain't got much time to lose. That Ramon gets there by two o'clock.'

They had not much time to lose, but they had in theory enough. Buses from outside the college ran at twenty-minute intervals, the journey to the professor's took only half an hour or a little more, and it was only just a quarter to one.

But.

But bus services everywhere suffer from shortage of staff, and when they do they are apt simply to miss out one particular run. The run missed that day was the one due to pass the college at 1 p.m. exactly. That need not have mattered. The 1.20 would bring them to within a couple of hundred yards of the professor's by five minutes to two at the latest. And it arrived at the college on the dot.

And, in the words of its conductor, it 'suffered a mechanical breakdown' just five minutes later.

Mrs Craggs hopped out in an instant and posted herself plonk in the middle of the road. In less than a minute a car had to pull to a halt in front of her. An irate lady motorist poked her head out. Mrs Craggs marched up to her.

'Life an' death,' she said. 'It may be a matter o' life an' death. We gotter get to Halliman's Corner before two o'clock.'

The lady motorist, without a word, opened the car's door. Mrs Craggs, Mrs Milhorne and Rosita piled in. Once on the go, Mrs Craggs explained in more detail. The lady motorist grew very excited. But she was a lady who relied more on the feel of the countryside than on signposts or maps. And a quarter of an hour later all four had to admit they had no idea where they were.

'The telephone,' suggested the lady motorist. 'We shall have to go to a house and telephone your professor.'

'No good,' said Mrs Craggs. 'He don't never answer it when he's working. Rare old miracle he is like that. Ring, ring, ring an' never a blind bit o' notice.'

'I'd die out o' curiosity,' put in Mrs Milhorne.

'So would I, dear,' said Mrs Craggs. 'But that ain't getting the cavalry to the wagon train.'

They resumed their progress then, eyes strained to catch the least sign of anything helpful. And it was Mrs Craggs who spotted something.

'That old plastic sack on top o' that gatepost,' she said. 'I remembers it from the bus coming out. It's that way. To the left. That way.'

The lady motorist, recognising an infallible sign when she met one, turned at once.

'We'll be there in five minutes,' she shouted.

'Yes,' answered Mrs Craggs. 'An' it's two minutes to two now.'

There was a little argument about whose watch was rightest, but all agreed that two o'clock was bound to come before their destination. And it did.

'Quick,' said Mrs Craggs, as at last they got to the familiar corner. 'Up that way. We may not be too late. He may not've done it yet.'

But she could not see in her mind's eye that prowling jaguar stopping to mow the old professor's lawn before he struck. What she could see, all too clearly, was the thorn-like, obstinate old man defending his property to the last. And she could see frail thorns, spiky though they might be, all too easily being crushed to splinters.

The car pulled up with a screech of brakes. Mrs Craggs was out of it before it had stopped. She hurled open the gate. The garden was empty. Ominously empty. Mrs Craggs tore across the unmown lawn like an avenging Amazon. She burst into the professor's study.

The professor was sitting holding up an ancient coin, scrutinising it with extraordinary care.

'Ramon,' Mrs Craggs burst out. 'Where's Ramon?'

Professor Partheman turned to her.

'Ah, yes, Ramon,' he said. 'Well, Mrs Craggs, I happened to read in *The Times* this morning a most interesting article about research at John Hopkins University in America proving that women have particular skill in what is called non-verbal communication. Or, to put it in popular terms, their instinct is to be trusted. So, with that fact at my disposal, I decided to give credence to your – ahem – feeling, and I left a note on the gate telling Ramon I no longer required his services and at the same time I had a word with our local constable.'

He rubbed his fleshless old hands together briskly.

'Yes, Mrs Craggs,' he went on, 'one can trust a woman's intuition. One can trust it for a fact.'

'Yes, sir,' said Mrs Craggs.

Goodbye, Mrs Milhorne. Goodbye. I'm going now. Do finish your pot of tea, and the cakes. But goodbye. Yes, goodbye.

... an', as I was saying, you couldn't call Elma Craggs no modern woman. I mean, not like what I am. I mean, feminist, she ain't never heard the word. But I go in for that, I do. In a ladylike way, mind. What I say is, you gotter be refined whatever you do. But Elma Craggs, she just goes on being a woman, if you take my meaning.

What, gone, 'ave you? Well, I mean to say. Not what I call very ladylike behaviour, not very television like. Just to get up an' go, and me come all the way from Lord's. Well. Well, I never.

XIV

Caught and Bowled, Mrs Craggs

MEMBERS OF THE MARYLEBONE CRICKET CLUB do not drop toffee papers on the floor of the Long Room at Lord's. Nevertheless during the course of a day's hard cricket-watching a certain amount of debris does appear on that wide expanse of marbled brown linoleum. So it has to be cleared up.

Which is how it comes about that that stretch of territory sacred by long tradition to the male of the species, sub-genus cricket-lover, is trodden daily by Mrs Craggs, cleaning lady, and her friend Mrs Milhorne, cleaning lady too if of a more refined sort.

But not only does Mrs Craggs vigorously sweep and yet more vigorously polish early in the mornings well before play begins (Mrs Milhorne does rather more artistic things with a feather duster), but later in the day in some cavern measureless to man within the Pavilion both these examples of womanhood are still actually to be found on the premises, chiefly cutting sandwiches.

And it was a good thing, on this particular day, that Mrs Craggs, female though she is, was there. Otherwise a murderer might have carried his bat all the way till the last great stumps are drawn.

It was the third day of the Test. England were battling with a small lead on the first innings and four wickets cheaply down. A good hour before the Indians were due to come out on to the field some of the older, more regular, more passionately devoted Members began to gather in the Long Room. In various ways, more or less sly, they set about bagging their favourites among those specially made, high-seated bentwood chairs that are ranged in front of the wide expanse of window looking out at the field of play.

To be in the sun on the terraced Pavilion steps was all right for youngsters who could still take the heat. But with advancing years the cool of the Long Room was the place for them, and the window chairs.

And for most of these early comers the years had advanced to an extraordinary extent, without, of course, in any way abating their fanatical interest in the game. There was the Member Who Saw Grace's Last Century, generally called Grace's Last for convenience. Even more ancient was a favourite of Mrs Craggs's, the Oldest Member but Three, a tortoise-like old boy never seen except in the season, never seen except in a frayed-sleeved blazer and time-creased MCC tie. He was apt to be called But Three.

Indeed, proper names were seldom used in this circle. If it wasn't something connected with cricket, it was a nickname deriving from some disgraceful episode at a prep school in the early years of the century, like Boggers or Winkie. Or it was just 'That Feller in Wine'. Or 'The Yorkshire Chap', a Member who perversely delighted in extolling Northern cricketers in this Middlesex stronghold.

And it was the Yorkshire Chap who began it all. He came striding up the Pavilion's wide stone stairs, wearing, of course, a Yorkshire blazer together with his MCC tie (ties and jackets, thank heaven, are still mandatory in the Long Room), his ruddy bald head already glistening with sweat and his big belly protruding in front of him like a dangling sack of flour. And as soon as he saw the others he started holding forth.

'I bet you one thing,' he said, his voice reverberating from one end of the room by the painting of old Thomas Lord himself right down to the other where Don Bradman has been caught by the artist wearing a business suit and so looking, without white flannels and long-peaked green cap, like an utter fish out of water.

'I bet you one thing. I bet anybody here a hundred pound straight that there's a Yorkshireman's century before today's play's done.'

There was a stir of interest among the little group he had addressed. Mrs Craggs, who at this very early hour was still within hearing of the Long Room, her polishing mop in hand, noticed it at once.

'But then,' she said later to Mrs Milhorne down among the sandwiches, 'money's money. It means something, money does. Not like all this scoring, an' centuries, an' leg before whatsit.'

'Oh, I like cricket,' Mrs Milhorne replied. 'I love it. Reely. All kind of restful. More like the bally, I always think. Like nice slow dancing. Romantic. I always was romantic, you know.'

Perhaps it was a good thing that the two of them were buried deep. If one of the Members had heard … But Mrs Craggs paid it all no attention.

'Yes,' she said, 'an' they took 'im up, they did. Every blessed one o' the old boys sitting together there. Seemed to think they was on to a good thing. "Why," said one of 'em, "the wicket's turning and your feller's still fiddling about in his twenties, he'll never do it." Don't know what he meant. That old wicket ain't turned to left nor right, far as I can see.'

'Oh, but he's right,' said Mrs Milhorne. 'I saw the headlines this morning. "England in Trouble", they said. I like that, I do. Old England's always at her best when there's trouble.'

Mrs Craggs thought of saying a word or two about Mrs Milhorne always being at her most depressed whenever a mite of trouble came her particular way. But she decided to be charitable. Besides, if she had spoken, Mrs Milhorne would have been at her pills in a moment, and then she'd be so dopey she'd never even get two sandwiches put together, never mind butter forty dozen.

So she pursued the theme of money rather than that of cricket. 'Mind you,' she said, 'there'll be trouble about those bets. I can smell it. A hundred pound either way. It don't match up to what it's all about. No wonder they call this the Nursery End, just a lot o' kids they are.'

'Oh, but gentlemen like them,' Mrs Milhorne protested. 'A hundred pounds don't mean nothing to them, not reely. It just shows they're interested, reely interested in the game.'

'Trouble,' Mrs Craggs replied tersely. 'Trouble. Mark my words.'

And indeed those bets were to be won and, in an altogether extraordinary way, lost too before play was over at Lord's that day. And murder was to be committed in the Long Room.

* * *

Members of the Marylebone Cricket Club do not use the Long Room at Lord's as a common betting shop. Nevertheless when the great game of cricket rouses passions to a fever heat the verb 'I bet' can sometimes be heard. As it had been on the day murder was committed in the Long Room.

But that day seemed at its beginning tranquil enough. The headlines in the papers promising trouble for England did not prove exactly factual. The Indian bowlers were turning the ball a little and they toiled hard. But England steadily piled on the runs with the Yorkshireman distinctly aggressive.

So as it neared the lunch interval a Yorkshire century began to look very likely. In the Long Room the Yorkshire Chap was openly jubilant, and his companions were finding it hard to keep looking sanguine.

Mrs Craggs, emerging for a breather from that deep cavern where sandwiches are cut (Mrs Milhorne had irritated her beyond endurance by refusing to work at the cheese variety on obscure medical grounds), spotted the Oldest Member But Three on this way to answer a call of nature looking really very glum indeed.

'Poor old duck,' she said to Mrs Milhorne, 'trotting off

down there, trotting back again, not wanting to miss a single moment of it – an' nothing really happening as far as I can make out. Him an' his grimy old striped tie, been round his neck for fifty years by the look of it.'

'It's that Yorkshire one I can't stand,' Mrs Milhorne replied, without much logic. 'You can hear his voice right down here when he comes out. On about cheese sandwiches he was just now. Someone asked him if he wanted one for lunch. And you should have heard him saying no. Great healthy fellow like him. You'd of thought they was offering poison, you would.'

'I dare say there's some as'd like to do that,' Mrs Craggs said, with a chuckle. ''E's not exactly top o' the pops in there, the Yorkshire Chap.'

'No,' Mrs Milhorne agreed. 'Someone suggested a nice bit of Wensleydale just now. That's a Yorkshire cheese, and he ought to of liked it. But, do you know, I had to come right back down here to get away from his language. Right back down here.'

Mrs Craggs, who had suspected that her companion had not been hard at work during her absence, pursed her lips at this unwitting confirmation. But before she had a chance to comment something else distracted her attention.

She listened for a moment to sounds coming from the direction of the bar behind the Long Room. Then, instead of going back to the sandwiches, she moved a few paces nearer, regardless of the fact that in doing so she was intruding a female presence into at least semi-sacrosanct territory.

Then, as a waiter carried into the Long Room a tray on which there were half a dozen glasses and two bottles of wine, Italian wine in straw-covered plump bottles, she did something altogether unprecedented. She marched, feminine flowered apron flaunting, right into the Long Room itself.

The very moment she crossed the threshold, just under the disapproving look of old Thomas Lord himself, there was a stir of protest. She was quite well aware of it, but she tramped on. Straight up to the end of the long table where the Yorkshire Chap and his fellow cricket-lovers were gathered she went. And she looked the Yorkshire Chap full in the face.

'You're not to touch a drop o' that,' she said, pointing a lean brown finger at the two fat bottles of wine. 'Not a —'

She got no further. The Yorkshire Chap rose from his chair, big belly looming up like the first hint of an undersea atomic explosion, drew in a single deep breath and pronounced.

'A woman,' he said, voice bouncing off the glass cases of ancient bats and brownish shrivelled historical balls. 'You're a woman.'

''Course I'm a woman,' Mrs Craggs retorted. 'Do I look like I was anything else?'

And it was true that, if no longer the pretty girl who had, forty and more years before, captivated a certain Alf Craggs, she was still, crinkled and creased though her nut-brown face had been by the hard years, undoubtedly a woman. But women are not, are simply not, permitted in the Long Room, and in a minute a couple of post-war Members had politely swept her out.

She would not have let it happen, though. Only, as she went, she was able to hear the loud voice of the Yorkshire Chap demanding 'a bottle of decent burgundy, not this Italian pigswill'. And she even half-heard That Feller in Wine, who had been kind enough to stand his friends a rather good Chianti for lunch, murmur an unavailing protest.

And then, when the Yorkshire bat out in the sun-kissed field had got to within one run of his century and had struck there, the umpires called for lunch. Still, it looked as if the big swaggering Yorkshire Chap's money was as safe as if it was already in the bank. Yet it was not.

Not that, with the second ball after lunch, the 99 on the score-board wasn't transformed with a sizzling four between the covers to 103. But by that time the Yorkshire Chap was dead, a dramatic seizure had laid him flat, his head just resting against one of the tall semi-circular wastepaper baskets on the back wall of the room, emptied that very morning by Mrs Craggs herself. So, of course, the bets were cancelled.

Down below, Mrs Craggs was taking a cuppa before pushing

off home. When she heard the news she turned to Mrs Milhorne and said, 'Very convenient for some too, dear, 'im going like that. You know, I think I'll just stay on for a bit.'

* * *

Members of the Marylebone Cricket Club do not expire on the floor of the Long Room at Lord's. Some things simply are not done. Except that occasionally they happen.

As death happened that third day of the Test to the man they called the Yorkshire Chap. So, quickly as they could, they scouted round for a doctor who was a Member. But no one was available, and at last after a loudspeaker appeal they had to make do with a young medico with no real right to enter the Long Room at all.

However, he seemed to know his business and before long he was saying that it appeared to be a case of simple heart failure. Though there would have to be an inquest and some undesirable publicity, there should be no need now for anything more than a discreet and rapid removal of 'the – er – body'.

But then Mrs Craggs, who despite her undoubted feminineness had been summoned, a little after the doctor, to deal with the mess of spilled wine and broken glasses on the long polished table in the centre of the room, spoke up. 'Only it's murder,' she said.

'Don't talk nonsense, woman.' 'Just get on with the clearing up, Mrs Harumph.' 'I don't think there's any need for that sort of talk.' Replies were quick to come. And every one of them pretty sharp.

Which perhaps made Mrs Craggs only the more determined to be heard. 'Murder, I said, and murder I meant. Tell you what the weapon was, too.'

'My good woman, there was no weapon and no murder. This is just a case of sudden heart failure.' The young doctor summoned from the proletarian huddle of the lunchtime Tavern did not appreciate having his expert opinion called in question.

Mrs Craggs put her hands on her hips and regarded him squarely. 'The weapon was some wine what they call Chianti,' she told him. 'An' that's a fact.'

But, quite unexpectedly, at the mention of the name of this common and excellent Italian wine, the young doctor looked suddenly doubtful.

'Yes,' said Mrs Craggs. 'Chianti. Just look at them bottles with the straw stuff round 'em.'

'What the devil is the woman talking about?' said That Feller in Wine. 'Perfectly good Chianti that. Sell plenty of it myself.'

'Yes, of course, sir,' the young doctor replied. 'But I'm afraid it is true that in some circumstances Chianti can be a killer. If it's taken when you happen to be using what's called an MAOI anti-depressant. A few things react with those very strongly. Cheese, Chianti, Iranian or Russian caviar. Does anybody know if the gentleman was by any chance taking pills or tablets?'

No one replied. So Mrs Craggs spoke up again. 'He wouldn't touch cheese,' she said. 'My friend Mrs Milhorne heard him only today. Swore he wouldn't touch even a crumb o' Wensleydale, he did. That was when I tried to warn 'im about Chianti, an' got politely pushed out of here for me pains. 'Cept I did hear him order something else.'

'But how did *you* know Chianti can be dangerous?' the doctor demanded, a little nettled.

'My friend Mrs Milhorne,' said Mrs Craggs. 'Martyr to depression, she is. So she says. Wouldn't even touch the cheese for the sandwiches on account o' the pills she has. Told me about 'em many a time she has, all about 'em.'

But it was the MCC Secretary himself, called to the scene before even the doctor, who put the really important question. 'Tell me, Mrs Craggs,' he said, 'is it because you heard him order some other wine that you think his death isn't as simple as it looked?'

'Got it in one, sir,' Mrs Craggs said to this mighty personage. 'Old Yorkshire knew for a cert he must never touch that stuff. An' there were people in this room just going to lose hundred-pound bets. So ain't it likely that someone switched glasses on him? Ain't it, sir?'

And that was when the Secretary said that the very least they could do was to get in touch with Scotland Yard. And he added that perhaps it would be as well if nobody went home just yet.

But in any case, as the Oldest Member But Three pointed out, no one was going to go home at this juncture. England had really begun to knock up a commanding lead and the Yorkshireman's display was a joy to watch.

No one, however, was able to look on from those specially made high bentwood chairs in the Long Room. Now that such doubt had been cast on the manner of the Yorkshire Chap's death there could be no question of moving the body until the man from Scotland Yard had arrived.

So out into the heat on the steps in front of the Pavilion went all the little group who had been the Yorkshire Chap's companions during this momentous day, Boggers, Winkie, the Member Who Saw Grace's Last Century, the Oldest Member But Three and That Feller in Wine. Inside the Long Room only the Secretary and Mrs Craggs remained.

'Perhaps you could just clear up those glasses he knocked over, Mrs Craggs?' the Secretary suggested.

'I don't think as 'ow I'd better, sir,' said Mrs Craggs.

'Oh, come, I can't see any objection.' But Mrs Craggs shook her grey-curled head. 'Look at where he fell, sir. Right by that wastepaper basket there, yards away from the table. He never knocked no glasses over. Someone else did that. To hide that they'd switched glasses on him.'

And, sure enough, when a certain Detective-Superintendent Hutton arrived – he *would* share the name of that great cricketer on a case like this – he was quick to appreciate Mrs Craggs's point. He was more than ready, too, to take advantage of her sharp observations. ('It's on account of I keeps my eyes open for dust, sir.')

After quite a short conversation he was able to say, half to himself, half to this invaluable assistant he had acquired. 'So there were five of them with the deceased today, were there?

Just five. Well, I think I'd better see each one of them before I do anything else.'

* * *

Members of the Marylebone Cricket Club do not submit to police interrogation in the Long Room at Lord's. Unless there's been a murder in the Long Room.

But murder there had been – or at least a highly suspicious death – and Detective-Superintendent Hutton was decidedly interested in the five Members who had spent most of the victim's last hours in his company. The two whom Mrs Craggs had identified by their prep school nicknames, Boggers and Winkie, the one she knew as That Feller in Wine, and the two extreme ancients, the Oldest Member But Three and the Member Who Saw Grace's Last Century.

The superintendent was anxious to talk to them. But he did not share his unorthodox colleague's view on why any one of them might be a killer. 'Come now, Mrs Craggs,' he said. 'To take a life over a bet of a hundred pounds? I'm afraid it's just not on, you know.'

'If you say so, sir,' Mrs Craggs replied. 'But that Yorkshire Chap did die when those bets looked as if they was as good as money in his pocket. On 99 the feller out there was, one off that century. You can't get over that.'

Superintendent Hutton, who had clean bowled a fair number of murderers in his time, gave Mrs Craggs a smile which mingled a fair ration of sharp amusement with its outward kindliness. 'We'll see,' he said. 'But in the meantime there's nothing to stop you going off home now. Thanks very much.'

'As you say, sir,' said Mrs Craggs. But she did not go home. Instead she made her way to a quiet nook she knew of and there she sat and waited.

She had a long time to wait, too. Out on the green of the field England added run to run and the Indian bowlers slaved and sweated, neither side knowing that the death that had taken place in the Long Room at the lunch break had been anything other than an unfortunate incident. And in the cool of the Long Room Superintendent Hutton and his sergeant talked at length with each of five men.

Boggers – he turned out to be Major-General E.H. Fitzharding – agreed that he had had this 'rather foolish' bet with the dead man. 'Jolly sorry he isn't here to collect, actually.' But, no, beyond meeting him at Lord's from time to time he knew nothing about the chap.

Winkie – and he was Mr Arnold Boutley of the Foreign Office – said almost exactly the same. 'He was a good enough fellow in his way, you know. But naturally one didn't …'

The Oldest Member But Three, a Mr Charles Tilkinson, subjected to equally long, polite but persistent questioning, produced nothing more germane. 'I'm afraid I never actually knew his – er – name, you know. Funny thing, I suppose. But as one grows older …'

The Member Who Saw Grace's Last (Rear-Admiral Sir Horace Virtonbright, KCVO, CMG, DSO) was more forthright but no more informative. 'Bit of a bounder really. Man was a Member and all that. But. Well, there it is.'

That Feller in Wine, or Mr Frederic Lowesmith, managing director of Lowesmith and Lowesmith, Duke Street, St James's, did have a little more to contribute. He had after all bought the circle the Chianti that looked as if it had been, as Mrs Craggs had called it, the murder weapon. 'Do you know, Superintendent, I've been in the wine trade all my life, and my father before me, and I had no idea Chianti did that, not the least notion.'

But he was unable, like the others, to recall anything about what exactly had been happening at the table before suddenly the Yorkshire Chap had lunged forward, sent all the glasses crashing over and had died.

'He lunged forward, did he?' Superintendent Hutton asked quickly. 'Knocked over the glasses?'

Mr Lowesmith thought for a moment. 'Well, no, Superintendent, I'm not sure that he did. I seem to remember actually that he fell backwards. Yes, I'm sure he did. But then …?'

'You didn't see anyone knock over the glasses afterwards? Perhaps in the excitement of it all?'

'No. No, I'm afraid I didn't. You see, we were all looking at – at the poor chap.'

And though the questioning had gone on for some time after this, just as it had gone on with the others, apparently the superintendent felt that he could get no further. A little later, tucked away in her nook, Mrs Craggs heard his sergeant telling everybody that they could now go.

Which was when she emerged, pushed past the sergeant without so much as a by-your-leave and went straight up to the superintendent. 'Sir,' she said, 'there's something I got to put you right about.'

The superintendent looked at her, plainly a good deal irked.

'It's Mrs Craggs, isn't it?' he said. 'I did tell you it was all right for you to be off, you know. Quite some time ago.'

'Yes,' said Mrs Craggs, 'you did. An' you told all the rest of 'em it's all right for them to go too. Well it ain't, you know. It bloody ain't. You're letting go a murderer, an' I can tell you which of 'em it is.'

* * *

Members of the Marylebone Cricket Club do not get arrested for murder in the Long Room at Lord's. Unless, of course, it becomes apparent to an investigating officer while the Member is answering a few extra questions in the Long Room that he has actually committed a murder.

And provided too, of course, that the investigating officer has been lucky enough to have been assisted by Mrs Craggs, cleaning lady. However unwillingly it had been at first.

'Mrs Craggs,' Superintendent Hutton had said when she had pushed her way in and told him it wasn't bloody right for him to let go one of the five men who had made bets with the dead Yorkshire Chap in the Long Room that morning. 'Mrs Craggs,

I dare say I owe something to your gift of observation, but I think you've long ago told me all you can.'

'Oh, no, I ain't. You didn't ask, so I didn't say. Thought you'd likely find out for yourself. That's what I thought then.'

'Find out what? Have you been withholding evidence? Because if so, let me warn you, you have been committing a very serious offence.'

'I wasn't withholding no evidence,' Mrs Craggs replied. 'I wasn't withholding one thing you couldn't of seen for yourself. If so as you'd opened your eyes and looked.'

The superintendent's face froze then in an anger that had reduced many a junior in rank to abject silence, let alone many an outright villain. But it failed altogether to silence Mrs Craggs.

'Didn't you see?' she demanded. 'Didn't you see what was in front of your very eyes? 'Cos if you didn't you should be polishing this 'ere floor an' trying to get the dirt out of them little stud marks everywhere, an' I should be a-lording it down Scotland Yard.'

The insult ought to have had Mrs Craggs bundled out of the Long Room in less time than it takes to tell, and much less gently than she had been bundled out when she had tried to warn the Yorkshire Chap not to drink Chianti. But Superintendent Hutton had not notched up his half-century of caught murderers by being pig-headed.

'There was something to see, was there?' he asked with a sudden change-down in tone. 'Well, suppose you tell me just what that was, Mrs Craggs.'

There was more menace in his quietness than there had been in his anger, and for once Mrs Craggs sounded defensive when she answered.

'Well, I s'pose you never did see him stuff that old score-card into his shoe, same as I did once when he thought nobody wasn't looking,' she said.

'Stuff a score-card into his shoe? What on earth are you saying, woman?'

A glint of the sardonic came into Mrs Craggs's eyes in

response. All right if he couldn't see it when it was practically thrust under his nose ...

'What you think a person would put a thick sheet o' paper into his shoe for?' she demanded. ''Cos he's got a hole in the sole, o' course. An' why would he have a hole in the sole of his shoe? 'Cos he couldn't afford to have 'em mended. An' if he couldn't afford that, he couldn't afford to fork up a hundred quid, could he? An' he'd gone an' made that bet, hadn't he? In the excitement o' the moment. Cricket mad as he is.'

But now Superintendent Hutton, who could after all very easily see a thing if it was thrust under his nose, was absolutely with her.

'Of course,' he said. 'That grimy old tie. And his blazer. The sleeves of his blazer were frayed. I saw them. Saw them, but I never thought that a Member of the MCC didn't actually have to be well off. Of course, it's him.'

'Yes, dear,' said Mrs Craggs. 'You got it. Now. The Oldest Member But Three, poor old devil.'

But it was Superintendent Hutton who had the last word. He coughed once, and then he said:

'Thank you, Mrs Craggs.'